Carlton Dawe

Mount Desolation

An Australian romance

Carlton Dawe

Mount Desolation
An Australian romance

ISBN/EAN: 9783337315764

Printed in Europe, USA, Canada, Australia, Japan

Cover: Foto ©Andreas Hilbeck / pixelio.de

More available books at **www.hansebooks.com**

MOUNT DESOLATION.

AN AUSTRALIAN ROMANCE.

BY

W. CARLTON DAWE,

AUTHOR OF "THE GOLDEN LAKE," "SKETCHES IN VERSE," ETC.

CASSELL & COMPANY, LIMITED:

LONDON, PARIS & MELBOURNE.

1892.

To

NANCE

THIS BOOK

IS

AFFECTIONATELY INSCRIBED.

CONTENTS.

CHAPTER I.

CHAPTER II.

CHAPTER III.

CHAPTER IV.

CHAPTER V.

CHAPTER XIV.

MOUNT DESOLATION.

CHAPTER I.

BEFORE THE CURTAIN.

THE sun, a dull, red, angry ball of fire, was sinking slowly behind the jagged peaks of Mount Desolation, flooding the great black rocks with an indescribable glory, and casting gaunt fantastic shadows on the plains below. The grasshoppers clicked loudly in the long grass, and the little lizards crept further out upon the granite ledges to escape the lengthening shadows. Above, in the steel-blue sky, whirled flocks of noisy parrots, while close to earth the air was filled with the hum of countless insects, all sighing, as it were, for the setting of that god which was their life. Shrill laughed the merry jackass; the magpie chattered to its heart's content before it tucked its knowing head away beneath its wing; the blue bird and the "more-pork" had their say, the wombat crept from its hole to take a last peep, and the rabbit stopped in his head-long flight to look up at the great red god. The air, still warm, though tempered by approaching night, was laden with the perfume of wattle and honeysuckle, making it so delicious to inhale that one ceased to wonder why speechless Nature sobbed aloud. One great inarticulate cry went up to heaven; the sun sank behind the jagged peaks, and the silence of night fell upon the great plains.

Mount Desolation, as its name implies, was not in itself a very exhilarating object, being, in fact, a most gruesome and awe-inspiring monster. It was a huge barren mass of granite, rising some thousand feet above its surrounding alps—a thing of grim splendour and fascinating desolation. Seamed with deep black chasms, and strewn with iron-like boulders as slippery as blocks of ice, it presented formidable obstacles to its would-be assailant; and the people in the little town at its base rarely tempted fortune on its heights, but looked up from their thresholds at its great frowning brow and owned it master. To the children of the neighbourhood it was as mysterious as some mystic mountain of fairy lore, and they peopled its chasms with the ghosts of bygone generations of blacks, and with the presence of those immortals which we call sprites; and when the great white clouds rested on its grim summit, they used to say that God had come down to look upon his world. Oh, yes, there are children who dream even in the land of the Southern Cross, though their dreams have yet to be interpreted to them. The beauty we know so well is always the loveliest in our eyes. The strain of an old familiar song is the sweeter in our ear for our knowledge of its every note. The beauty of the earth is enhanced by guide-books.

Burke, the great explorer, who so soon after was to meet a fearful death away at Cooper's Creek, was the original discoverer of this strange mountain, and from him it received its gloomy title. He had marched many days in the hope of finding the promised land, but upon climbing this forbidding mount such a scene of desolation met his view that he named the hill accordingly. But many a long, long year has passed since then, and grimy men with picks and shovels have scrambled over its every accessible part in search of gold; and those long-stretching, cheerless plains are now dotted with sheep and cattle; roads cut them at right angles, and the train to Sydney passes thirty miles to the south-west. Indeed, the member for this district, Mr. Martin Wingrove, has promised its inhabitants that they shall have a branch line running right up to the foot of the mountain, ay, right into Desolation itself, for such is the name of the township which nestles at the foot of the great black hill.

This village, or town, of Mount Desolation—for in Australia all villages are towns—was situated on the banks of a little stream which went by the name of the Warrigal (tradition telling of the native belief that a great black Warrigal was the deity of the stream), and had seen some strange scenes since the day Burke first looked down upon its site. At one time its ambition soared to that of chief town of the northeast, and when gold was discovered, and the diggers poured in by hundreds, it felt as though it were about to achieve that distinction. But alas for its hopes! The rush was but a poor thing after all. Two or three rich veins were discovered, but the alluvial diggings were not worth the trouble of working. Then began a general exodus; only those who had neither inclination nor power to move staying on. But with a cheerful heart the inhabitants turned from gold-digging to agriculture and pastoral farming, as a less precarious if comparatively unexciting method of subsistence; and upon the bosom of those bleak far-stretching plains, which seemed so ghastly and forbidding to the early explorer, thousands of sheep and cattle pastured, and the district had the reputation of being in a very flourishing condition.

Yet upon occasions there was much life even in Desolation, as its inhabitants called it—not, apparently, having time to use the word Mount—especially on Saturdays and race weeks. Any place in Australia that pretends to consideration can boast its race-course, and it was not likely that such a thriving town as Desolation was going to be behind the times. As well might the mountain fall upon it and sweep it into chaos. It might boast of wealth, of luxury and learning, but unless it could also boast a racecourse it could have no pretensions to civilisation. It must have big names, too, for its races, such as Derby, Oaks, St. Leger; everything that could lend dignity to the gathering was freely patronised. And one week in every year the old town filled with strangers to partake of the local triumph. Traps rattled through the usually desolate streets, or street (for like most of its kind it had only one street of any consequence), and merry bushmen, mounted on their merry nags, galloped up and down with a recklessness which was simply charming. All the surrounding youth, beauty, and old age never missed the golden opportunity of attending this local fête, and if they did not make merry, the empty bottles we saw in the yard of the Mount Desolation Hotel must have borne false witness. It is true the thoroughbreds were not always of the highest class, nor the jockeys always sober, but that, instead of detracting from the enjoyment, considerably enhanced it. And didn't the bookmakers come all the way from Melbourne? and didn't they smoke big cigars, drink champagne, and flash their diamonds and bank-notes like a set of kings? And if the Desolationites failed to pocket any of those greasy notes, was it not entirely their own fault for backing the wrong horse? Ah, they were splendid times, as anyone would tell you, and the doings of one meeting

B

supplied sufficient anecdotes to keep the good people
going till the next.

But even when there were no races, the main street
of the township presented a very cheerful appearance
every Saturday night. Then the miscellaneous members of the community sought the refreshing atmosphere of the numerous bars, and in large quantities
of vile beer and viler spirits beguiled the evening hours.
On Sunday it was Desolation indeed ; but on Monday
the week began again, and the good folks laboured long
and early, in the broiling sun, in the pitiless rain—for
these people know how to work once they begin in
earnest. Surely after such a week of terrible toil no one
is sour enough to grudge them a little relaxation, even
though it take the form of beer and tobacco, and discourse of an unintellectual nature. They are happy
enough, heaven knows ; and though they live far from
the busy haunts of men, though their very existence is
unknown to the majority of their countrymen in the
south, they yet know themselves to be free-born
Australians with a splendid heritage, and that should
be enough for any man—especially when he can see
horse-racing once a year, and every Saturday night
of his life get gloriously drunk.

From this it must not be thought that all the
inhabitants of this cheerful spot live but for Saturday
night. A thousand times, no ! There is a strong
religious sentiment running through a large section of

the community, which community, being mostly of the Methodist persuasion, has an uproarious way of its own of showing that sentiment. They never attend a racecourse; never patronise the "Wombat's Head" or the "Bounding Kangaroo." The travelling circus tempts them not; the wandering Christy cracks his bones and rattles his tambourine in vain. They are the elect—they will tell you so a thousand times a day. All others are rushing to perdition. Their self-assurance, their unbounded egotism is a marvel, of which the world has not seen a greater. And there can be no doubt of their sincerity—they talk so much about it. The benighted Catholic may sneer, the ungodly Protestant smile in his atheistical way; but as the Son of Man was reviled, so shall His followers be.

And yet these good folks, if the rumours of the ungodly be worthy of credence, are as full of errors as the rest of poor humanity. They do not attend the races, nor the circus, nor the show of the bone-clapping Christy, but they do many other things of which we dare not speak lest we should be accused of setting down aught in malice. The cloak of charity has been said to cover a multitude of sins; the cloak of sanctity has likewise its advantages, as we have seen in these times, and in times gone by. Even these excellent Methodists, with all their prayers and hymns, have found that out. The contemplation of the spiritual does not always exalt the material, and the elected one is only a poor passionate piece of earth, into which the Superior Force has blown a puff of human fire.

But enough of him. We had forgotten that the sun was sinking all this time, and that we have more important things to chronicle than the idle tittle-tattle of every pitiable clique in a wretched little country township.

CHAPTER II.

THE CURTAIN GOES UP.

THE sun was setting then, a sullen ball of fire, and its angry beams shot fair into the eyes of two young people who, with slow gait and troubled faces, were slowly wending their way towards the homestead which lay about a mile before them. He was speaking rapidly, with impatient gestures, the red light of the angry sun sparkling fiercely in his eyes. Now and again she would seize his great brown hand in her little gloved one and press it timidly, turning up to his face a pair of the sweetest dark eyes that Mr. Thomas Stanford had ever seen—at least, so that young gentleman thought, for every time she looked up to him he stooped suddenly down and kissed her full on those pouting red lips of hers, or on that smooth white brow over which her hair fluttered in the most wayward manner. She was a tall slender girl, with a rich dark complexion, ruddy and brown like a peach—the sort of complexion only seen with dark women. Her years were but one score, though she looked older, as most Australian girls do, thanks to hot winds and sun. Like the fruit of their native hills, the sun kisses them to perfection with quickness inconceivable. They seem to ripen even as one sits and watches. The child of to-day is the young woman of to-morrow. Ankle skirts and maternity go hand in hand.

Her companion was a tall, dark-complexioned, broadly-built young man of about seven-and-twenty —a typical Australian, active, hardy, sport-loving, blunt, but honest as the day. Features somewhat sharp, and eyebrows slightly compressed, as though their owner had been in the habit of knitting them whenever in thought. This gave a somewhat fierce and eager look to his face, but instead of detracting from it, lent to it a look of command which heightened the general excellence of his well-cut features. White teeth gleamed from beneath a brown moustache, and out from all shone, in strange contrast to the general determination of his carriage, a pair of soft grey eyes. Yet even these, though they had been likened to a woman's on more than one occasion, had been known to shoot forth lightning sparks which, if they did not burn, at least were known to terrify. But, as a rule, they were soft, and even full of pity, and no one had ever been known to approach Tom Stanford with a tale of true distress without enlisting his sympathy.

What brought him to Mount Desolation no one ever knew or cared. It was known that he had come from somewhere on the Darling, but why, or from which part, was of no consequence. To Mr. Franklin, however, the father of the young girl by his side, he had presented excellent credentials, and was employed as manager of the station, in which capacity he had given entire satisfaction. As we have said, no one had questioned whence he came or what he was, but, for certain reasons which shall be seen hereafter, he volunteered all information respecting his birth and parentage for his employer's benefit. So from that source we learn that his father was at one time a merchant in Sydney, but that reverses coming upon him, he was forced to the seclusion of a small country house which he had managed to save from the wreck of his fortune. Here Master Thomas, then a boy of twelve, dwelt with his parents for the next five years. Then both mother and father followed each other to the grave, after an interval of five months, and Tom, now a big strapping fellow of seventeen, was sent back to Sydney and put in his uncle's office. Office work, however, suited not his active nature, and after eighteen months of it he prevailed upon his uncle to let him go into the country to learn the pastoralist's trade, his ultimate object being to take up some land on his own account. So into the country he went with a friend of the family, a man who owned a big run away up near the Queensland border, and after a two years' sojourn in those parts he packed up his swag and came farther south. From that time he roamed hither and

thither at his own sweet will, for Master Thomas had
something of the nomad in him, till he was brought
up with a round turn, as a sailor would say, at Mr.
Franklin's station of Koorabyn. Here he proved himself both clever and assiduous, and if he was a little
reckless at times Mr. Franklin purposely shut his
eyes. There was reckoned no better rider than he on
the Darling, and sure no bolder one was ever seen.
Buckjumper or bullock, it was all one to him; and a
story was told of his having ridden a wild bull for a
wager, and won it too. Therefore, when he first came
to Mount Desolation he fairly astonished the natives
—a race of reckless riders. Horses that no one else
could sit he sat and tamed, and when he rode at
the races his mount always carried the most money
It was here his reputation for daring increased, and
when they saw him ride into the town of a Saturday
afternoon, with big Joe Devine, his constant companion, by his side, the people knew there was going
to be some fun down at the " Bounding Kangaroo,"
for to that alcoholic retreat the " bloods" of Desolation
adjourned for fun and frolic. Some of the virtuous
ones to whom we have referred, to whom cakes and
ale were an abomination, had approached Mr. Franklin
on Stanford's behalf, but as Mr. Franklin had found
no fault with that young gentleman, but had proved
him to be a most excellent overseer, their visits produced no effect. Besides, no matter what he might

do at the " Bounding Kangaroo," he was never absent from his duties, and that, in his employer's eyes, was a virtue which outweighed his petty vices.

But of a sudden this dissipation ceased. One Tuesday afternoon he drove the trap over to the railway station to meet Miss Alice Franklin, who was coming back from Melbourne after an absence of several years. Mr. Franklin had often spoken to the young manager of his beautiful daughter, and had naturally excited that young man's imagination. At last the news came that she was really coming, and as Mr. Franklin happened to be rather unwell on the day of her arrival, he deputed Stanford to go and fetch her in his stead. Tom was on the platform when the train steamed in; he saw a pretty, fashionably-attired young lady step from a first-class carriage, and as she was the only woman who had alighted, he knew it must be she for whom he had been sent. For the first time in his life Mr. Stanford grew exceedingly nervous. He stood staring at her like a big fool, and it was not till she approached and asked him if he had come from Mr. Franklin that he could find his tongue. But the drive back was pleasant enough for all that. He had seen little of ladies for many years now, and this young girl came like a revelation to him. Was there ever such a sweet voice? he wondered, and he sat listening to her musical prattle like one in a dream. And how she did talk, in her soft cultured way!

What a string of questions she asked, never waiting
for a reply! Oh, yes—thus went her prattle—she had
been to school at Melbourne, but not for the last two
years. During that period she had been " out." She
had not been to Koorabyn for ever so long—not since
she was fifteen. She was twenty now. Fancy!—
wasn't she getting old? Was Jura, the kangaroo dog,
still alive? My word, how he could jump! And
didn't he have a horrible scar right down his face
which a nasty old man kangaroo had once done in a
fight? Dead, was he?—poor old Jura! "We called him
Jura, you know, because he was so big, and there is a
big mountain somewhere in Europe called by that
name. Papa has seen it. Of course papa is English,
and he knows all about those strange European places."
And how was papa? And were the quinces she had
planted five years ago still growing? She was awfully
fond of quinces. Injurious! Oh dear, were they?
She had often made her luncheon off a quince and a
slice of bread-and-butter. And a nice luncheon it
was, too! He ought to try it. He smiled and said
he would if she would give him a quince from one of
her trees. She looked at him and her chatter ceased
of a sudden. There was something so earnest in the
grey eyes that looked down into hers that she at once
relapsed into the " young lady." A rather irksome
silence followed, broken but little till the roof of
Koorabyn loomed in sight. All the same, Mr. Thomas

Stanford forgot to visit the "Bounding Kangaroo" the following Saturday night.

But time brings many changes, and since that memorable drive Miss Franklin and Mr. Stanford had become very dear to each other; and that is the chief reason why their faces look so anxious in the red glare of this day's setting sun.

"But, Tom," she was saying, "do you mean that papa has really turned you off—really, Tom?" She repeated the word as though she could scarcely grasp its meaning.

"Yes, really," he answered somewhat bitterly. "I am to go the way I came, and the place that knew me once shall know me no more for ever." He tried to make light of the occurrence, but there was a quiver in his voice he never meant should be there.

"But why, Tom, why has father done all this? I have heard him praise your energy and sense a hundred times; and he even wrote to me in Melbourne the most glowing accounts of his new manager. Now all is suddenly changed, and without a word of warning you are turned away as though you were some rogue or vagabond."

"Perhaps he thinks I am."

"He could not think that."

"You know there are some people in the district who would give me a very evil reputation."

"But that was long ago," she said.

" Before I saw you." He threw his arm round her and drew her to him. " There, there," he continued. " Let them say what they please. We love each other; what more should we want ? "

But this would not satisfy the girl, who, being an only child, and motherless, was naturally of a wilful disposition.

" I want to know what it means, Tom, and what you mean. As my father is not a madman, there must be some reason for your dismissal. What is it ? for you, at least, must guess."

" I do, and since you wish it I will tell you. The fact that I have served your father for three years without an angry word is, or should be, sufficient proof that I have served him well."

" There can be no doubt of that."

" During the whole of that period I have been his companion, his friend. Under my care the property, never a good one, has considerably increased in value. In fact, all that a man could do has been done by me. Yet, without a word of warning, I am informed that I had better look out for another place, as Mr. Franklin intends to manage the run himself. Now, as your father has never taken interest enough in his property to be able to manage it, you will easily see that there must be some other motive for my dismissal."

" Yes, yes, but what can it be ? "

" Can't you guess ? "

She shook her head.

"Are you quite sure?"

She looked up at him, blushing like a rose, and said in a low voice, "Can it be Mr. Wingrove?"

"I am glad you did not profess ignorance. Yes, it is Mr. Wingrove, for it can be no one else. The man admires you."

She tossed her pretty head disdainfully. "What of that?"

"Much, dear. When a man like Martin Wingrove sets his heart upon a thing it will go hard with him if he does not get it. He is rich, influential, unscrupulous. And in our case he has the power to press, to injure. I am afraid of him."

"Then, I suppose, you are also afraid of me?" she asked somewhat pertly.

"Almost. I sometimes think that I was never born to such good fortune, that I am living in a fool's paradise, and that I shall wake up one morning and find my Eve has flown. But you love me," he added hastily, almost excitedly; "you do love me, Allie?"

She buried her crimson face on his breast and whispered, "You know I do."

"But say it," he said, "say it."

"I love you, I love you."

He bent down and kissed her passionately, fiercely.

"By heaven," he said, as he strained her to him, "I'll kill him if he comes between us."

"Hush," she cried, putting her hand to his mouth, "you must not say such wicked things."

He seized the little gloved hand and pressed it to his lips.

"It is the gospel," he said earnestly. "You are all I have in the world, all I hope for; you are my life itself. There is nothing I would not do for your sake, be it sacrilege or crime. There can be for me no happiness, here or hereafter, except through you."

She clung to him thrilled, yet half afraid of his fierce words.

"You must not love like that. I am only a poor silly girl, utterly unworthy of such devotion. You should have been the lover of some grand fierce woman, not a poor little body like me."

He laughed in an odd sort of way, but said nothing.

In the meantime the sun had sunk, and the cloud of dull red gold that it had left in its wake began to slowly dissolve into the steely haze: the chirp of the parrots died away, and only the low humming of insects filled the air. Away ahead of them the great black mountain loomed up solemn and grand, like some awful spirit in a world of fire.

At last the girl, who had remained silent for some time, shut in a world of thought, turned to him with a nervous, inquiring look.

"I have been thinking, Tom, and I cannot see why

we should blame Mr. Wingrove for your dismissal. It is all very well to say that the horrid man is in love with me, and that he would dismiss you if he had the power; but he was not your master."

"Master, Allie!"

"Forgive me, dear."

"No, no, you are right. I am a slave, and master is the correct word. The only difference between me and the negro is that I may call my body my own. Well, Wingrove is not my master—I wish it were only that."

"What could be worse?"

"He is the master of my master."

"What do you mean by that?"

"Have you not heard, do you not know?"

"I have heard nothing, I know nothing. It is five years since I have been here. All the world seems changed since then. Even old Desolation yonder, who was the wonder and terror of my childhood, scowls more fiercely and looks far gloomier than he did in the old days. Did you notice what a weird thing it looked a moment ago as it loomed up through that cloud of fire?"

"I did," said Stanford, "and I thought of Dante's Hell."

"Yes, yes," she almost screamed, so excited did she get, "that is it—it is Hell. Have you never heard the legend of that mountain?"

"Never," he answered. The people of Mount Desolation knew as little of legends as they did of Greek.

"In the native tongue," she continued, apparently forgetting in her excitement aught else but the mountain, "it is called the Hill of the Dead. Long, long ago, when the inhabitants of this country lived and warred as civilised men do now, there was a very powerful chief who made war against the magicians who lived in the great ranges yonder. This chief had determined to overthrow the magicians, and with that object in view gathered together a vast army; but in the night, while the countless thousands lay wrapped in sleep, the magicians arose in their might, and tearing yonder great hill from its seat in the earth, they hurled it upon the sleeping camp."

"How did you come by that strange story?"

"It was told to me by an old blackwoman whom we had about the station when I was a little girl. And, moreover, she used to say that the mountain could foretell when any great event was at hand. When mother died she foretold it, as I have heard father say a hundred times; and before the great drought came she told us that the mountain had given a terrible warning."

"Really," said Stanford, now interested in spite of himself, and casting strange looks towards that grim iron mass, which nestled, as it were, in a great cloud of lurid fire; "but did she forget to tell you how you were to read the warning?"

"No, even that was explained, and I turned it into rhyme."

"You did?" said he admiringly. "Do you remember it?"

"Yes," she replied, and forthwith repeated the following verse:—

" When the Mount like a demon looms through the glare of a sullen fire,
The heart of the watcher shall weep for the loss of a soul's desire."

There was something uncanny in the tone of her voice, and he quivered in spite of himself, but with a laugh he said, " Why, you elf, you are as full of superstitions as an old-world peasant. The grim old mountain yonder may be the tomb of thousands, but the days of signs and omens are past, and we are here to make fate, not to bow to it."

" Of course it is silly," she said, " and I try to shake off the feeling; but somehow I think that my life will for ever be associated with that horrible mountain."

" Then the association shall be one of pleasure—a pleasant memory. It shall no longer be Mount Desolation to us, but Mount Hope; and the demon who sits enthroned in yonder grim fortress we'll transform into an angel; and the 'sullen fire' of your rhyme we'll change to the golden pathway along which our

c

aged feet shall walk to the home of eternal sunshine. There," he added, with a laugh, "isn't that a better view of the picture ? "

" I hope for our sakes it will be the true one. But you were to tell me something," she said, coming back to the point she had so abruptly quitted. " What is there between my father and Mr. Wingrove ?"

" Perhaps I ought not to tell you. Yet it will out sooner or later, and to you it can be no breach of confidence. Your father, then, is in Mr. Wingrove's power."

" How in his power ?"

" Mr. Wingrove holds a mortgage on Koorabyn. He is your father's friend, of course, and would take no advantage of the power he holds ; but, should he determine on striking, he could drive the master of Koorabyn forth as its master has driven me."

" Are you sure of what you say ?" she asked.

" Yes. I do not know the amount, but I know of it."

" Then the blackwoman's legend was no fanciful conceit ; the days of signs and omens are not past, and the mountain has renewed its warning."

" No, no," he cried, as he folded her to him, " the black's legend was an old woman's tale. We are to make our fate, as I said before, not leave it for others to fashion. Will you come with me, Allie ? We'll go to Melbourne, Sydney—anywhere you choose. I am not rich, but I am young and strong, and I'll work for you, dear, while I can stand. You shall never see that horrible mountain again, never know what it is to have a care, save such as heaven may be pleased to send. I will devote my whole life to you, and shall be amply rewarded in knowing you are happy. What do you say—will you, will you come with me ? "

She made no reply, but sobbed gently on his breast.

"Do you know," he continued, as he pressed his lips into her wayward hair, " I am beginning to grow half afraid of that man Wingrove. He has too much power, too much wealth, for me to contemplate him with serenity. He loves you in his own selfish way ; and he has good reason to hate me. Our grievance dates prior to your return. I threatened to horsewhip him once, and he has never forgotten it. That in itself was enough to make him my implacable enemy. He swore then that I should live to rue that day, and he is one who never forgets or forgives. I laughed at his threats then, but I can't laugh now. I do not fear him as man to man," he added suddenly, as though to remove any suspicion of his cowardice from her mind : " I fear no man alive ; but this secret power which has robbed me of my place, which may rob me of my hopes, my life, is what I dread. There is no combating wealth and power, Alice, unless with similar weapons. The poor man must go under. Was

c 2

it not Napoleon who said that 'God is always on the side of the big battalions'?"

"Do you not overrate this man's power? How can he possibly injure you who have done nothing wrong?"

"How has he injured me? How he will I cannot say; though if he fights me fairly he may wish he had never begun the contest. But you have not answered my proposal. Will you come with me?"

"But I am sure papa will never consent to our marriage—at least not yet," she added by way of a sop to her gloomy Cerberus.

He smiled in a grim sort of way. "That's why I want you to run away with me."

"Papa would never forgive me."

"Would that affect you so much?"

"Of course it would."

"Then you do not love me as much as I thought."

"I love you better than anyone in the world," she said, "though you are a cross, disagreeable old thing. But papa—he is my father, he has been good to me. I should be more ungrateful than you would have your wife if I were to treat him with such ingratitude."

"Quite true," he said. "I was wrong, forgive me."

"You may kiss our hand," she said, in her own queenly way. He seized it, carried it reverentially to his lips, and kissed it very earnestly. Then suddenly drawing her to him, he caught her in his strong arms, and showered a volley of kisses all over her face and hair; nor would he have released her then had she not declared that he was crushing her to death.

"You are too rough for anything," she panted, as he loosened his grasp. "Look at my hat and hair."

"Very pretty, both. But do you know, I'm half mad whenever I come near you."

"Really, Tom, you frighten me. You look so fierce and passionate at times that I'm sure I'm half afraid of you."

"Afraid of me," he laughed. "It is I who am afraid of you."

"Ah," she said, "why won't you trust me?" There was just a little echo of pain in her voice.

"I do—I will," he answered almost fiercely, "for if I lose faith in you I am lost indeed."

"Now you are beginning again," she said, holding up her finger with a roguish look.

"There, there," he replied, his eyes almost swimming with tears, "you know what you are to me. Let evil come when it may, I will stand beside you till you yourself say 'Go.'"

"And that will never be."

They walked on slowly till they came to the slip rails which led into the home paddock, and thence to the house. These Stanford let down and she stepped within. He replaced them again, barring himself, as it were, from her; for with his dismissal had come

the intimation that his presence would no longer be
welcome at Koorabyn.   Mr. Franklin had dealt in no
half-measures.   A month's wages were paid in lieu of
notice, and Mr. Stanford's belongings were removed in
a trap to the Mount Desolation Hotel.   The irksome
business was gone through in a very few minutes.
Stanford was too proud to inquire the cause of
his dismissal; Mr. Franklin, for reasons of his own,
said as little as possible.   Thus, what might have been
a very unpleasant incident was, through the pride of
one and the shame of the other, concluded with
courtesy, if with no great respect.

   "Good-bye, Allie," he said, as he hung over the
rails; "when shall I see you again?"

   "Soon, soon."

   "Ah," he continued, "if you could only love me
well enough to trust me, there would be none of
this parting—not till our sun set for ever."   And as
he spoke he instinctively gazed away to where loomed
the great mountain in its cloud of dying fire.   And
while he looked he thought the flame grew bright
with a weird unnatural glory, while the uncouth
mass took unto itself the form of some strange
creature, half human, half beast, yet wholly repugnant.
He turned from it with a fierce scowl.   The superstition which lies in all men had been touched.

   "Ah," she cried, "did you see it?"

   "See what?" he asked with a laugh.

"The mountain!"

" Why, child, what do you mean ?"

But she had gone without replying. He leant forward on the rail watching her hurrying figure with a strange beating at his heart. What could it mean, this legend of the mountain, this blackwoman's tale? But what an idiot he was even to question it! And yet, in spite of all, as Alice's form disappeared in the distance, he turned once more to the great forbidding thing, and found himself unconsciously repeating the rhyme she had spoken :—

"When the Mount like a demon looms through the glare of a sullen fire,
  The heart of the watcher shall weep for the loss of a soul's desire."

CHAPTER III.

FATHER AND DAUGHTER.

How long Stanford stood watching the grim mountain he could not say, but he saw the clouds of fire turn from red to pink, and pink to grey, and night spread its dark wings over the giant's sullen brow. Then his thoughts came back to earth, as thoughts will, and he bethought him of his horse in the neighbouring clump of trees, and his fifteen mile ride back to Mount Desolation—for lovers in the bush have often to ride much greater distances to see the girl of their heart. Just then, however, he felt a heavy hand laid upon his shoulder, and with something like an oath he swung suddenly round; but on seeing who the offender was his savage look turned to one of cordial greeting.

"Ah, Joe, where did you spring from?"

"I have been watching you for some time," replied the new-comer, with a merry twinkle in his big brown eyes.

"Indeed!" There was a tone of constraint, of sudden coldness, in the word which did not escape the man.

"Not for any spying purposes, matey, but because

I wanted to see you. I didn't like to come up when
you were with the young lady."

"I understand. Well, what's the news?"

"He's been there again." The man Joe nodded
towards Koorabyn as he spoke. "I saw him go,
black horse and all. Blest if I don't think that
animal has as much of the devil in him as his
master."

"You mean Wingrove?"

"Yes."

"Curse him!" The eyes of the speaker flashed
ominously—almost as ominously as the sullen glare
that went down behind Mount Desolation.

"I say curse him, too, if curses are any good;
though I'm afraid they don't count much. But,
matey,". he continued, "it's always better to mount
the wall than try and butt it down. Can't you—can't
you do it smart-like?"

"How, smart-like—what do you mean?"

Joe turned his big eyes full upon him, and replied in his brief way—for Mr. Devine was one
never given to much talk—"Wingrove's got the old
man in his power; Wingrove's got the dollars; Wingrove 'll win."

"I'll kill him first."

Joe passed his hand across his throat.

"Ay," said Stanford fiercely, reading the action,
"and swing for it too."

"Folly, matey. The price would be too great for the job. Take my advice and run off with the girl. I'll guarantee to get everything ready if she'll only go with you as far as Wooroota. Once you are man and wife you may defy a thousand Wingroves."

"She would not consent."

"Ask her. When a woman loves a man she'll do anything for him."

Stanford looked hard at his companion. Could he know, or was he merely philosophising? Truly, Joe was not often taken thus, though man is a born philosopher. He knew more of horses than women, and more of the Bush than either; yet, for all the humour of his brown eyes, and his affected carelessness, there was much more in big Joe Devine than he was credited with.

"I have asked her."

"And she refused?"

"She did."

Joe gave a long incredulous whistle. "Good lord!"

Could it be possible? She loved, she was willing to give her hand, yet was afraid. Where then was the love, or of what nature was it? Mr. Joseph Devine confessed himself at fault. Brought up to range the bush, as free as the air, as the sun itself, he had never, like the great statesman, narrowed his mind, but had considered all things both possible and

probable in such a mighty world. The vastness of his
native wilds had seemed to permeate his brain, con-
fusing him, no doubt, and yet enlarging his idea of
things at the same time. Having been his own
master since he was big enough to earn a dinner, he
had not, till lately, recognised that law which says
that a man shall not live only for himself. Indeed,
he had never heard of it. With his swag upon his
shoulder he would trudge the length of the land with
a cheerful and contented spirit so that he felt that he
was independent of the whole world; put him on a
horse under the same conditions and there never was
monarch so happy as he. Therefore it seemed to him
an incredible thing that any girl who loved a man
should treat that man's honourable proposals with
such scant courtesy, for he knew that if he loved a
woman he would fly to her in the face of the whole
world. And so he told himself that the love was
all on one side; that women were always the same,
and that the devil himself never knew how to take
them.

Mr. Joe was a natural philosopher—that is to say,
he was no bookworm—and his philosophy told him
that the most pleasure to be got out of life was
through the gratification of each particular fancy;
and though this may seem a selfish, a sybaritic thing
to the virtuous, to all who lead a self-sacrificing life
(and so many do, you know!) to him it seemed the

most natural thing in the world, the first great law of
nature. The man who did not make the best of life
was an imbecile; the woman who had not courage
enough to take the hand of him she loved and say,
"I am yours," was unworthy of the name of woman.
Yet Mr. Joe, ignorant though he was of it, had a
more self-sacrificing nature than is to be found in
nine-tenths of his species; and when the time came
for the sacrifice he thought it as natural as the less
momentous events of his existence.

Yet this refusal caused him a bitter pang, and he
entirely disbelieved in her affection for Stanford. He
muttered deeply beneath his breath, and had he not
dreaded his companion's resentment, it is probable
that he would have made use of some strong language
in his disparagement of the sex. But he knew too
well of the mad infatuation of his friend. Indeed,
he had never known anything like this madness, and
he used to wonder if this insane person were really
the Tom Stanford whom he first knew away up on
the Darling. Then there was no wilder, merrier lad
than he; ready with his fists or his purse; always
the first where danger lurked, or where frolic held
revel. Didn't he remember how they chased the
bushrangers across the Darling Downs, and took
them, too, after a stubborn fight? And once, when
the river overflowed, had not Tom plunged in to his
rescue and saved him from inevitable death? It was

flood-time on the Darling; the mighty river was like
a foaming sea. He could not swim; he suffered all
the agony of drowning. Struggling like a madman,
his giant strength availed him nothing. The fierce
water caught him in its circling arms and bore him
onward with triumphant roar. And then he knew he
was sinking, sinking. The water hissed savagely in
his face; all life seemed to leave him; he wondered
why he did not die. With an effort he opened his
eyes; the water still swirled about him, but by his
side, with a face as rigid as iron, was Stanford. For
a moment he thought they were both dead, both
floating away on the great river together; and then
he fainted like a girl.

From that day Devine was Stanford's, for good or
evil, body and soul, and they became fast friends.
He had no advantages of education; he was rough,
uncouth; but beneath his shaggy exterior Stanford
soon found so many excellent qualities that he
received his friendship with delight. As for Joe,
he fairly idolised his mate, not in a servile way,
mind you—though he knew Stanford had received
some favours from fortune of which he could not
boast—for he was any man's equal; at least so he
had been taught. But as friend for friend, he would
have laid down his life for the man who had rescued
him from a grave in the Darling. And once, when
Stanford was stricken down with fever, the faithful

fellow never left his side; and Tom knows well that
had not Joe nursed him so tenderly, that illness
would have been his last. Poor Tom! poor Joe!
Had it been so, it would have been better for ye
both.

When Stanford left the river, Joe accompanied
him. Together they rode the length and breadth of
the Riverina, putting their hands to whatever came
in their way. In this manner they crossed the
Murray at Albury and wandered on till they reached
the Billabong district—Joe's native place. Here
Stanford received an offer from Mr. Franklin of
Koorabyn, with what result we know. Here, also,
was Devine installed; and though he was proud of
his friend's position he never ceased to regret their
aimless wanderings through the Bush. Now, however, they were free again. With his friend's dismissal had also come his own—for he was known
to the powers that be as Stanford's Shadow—and
never a long-sentence prisoner felt more joy in
stepping out into the free air than did Joe Devine
when he received his wages and was told to go.
They would take their horses as before and make
the tour of the colony, perhaps cross over into South
Australia—who should say where they would not go
now that they were free! Free! But were they?
We have seen enough to show us that Mr. Thomas
Stanford was anything but free; and when Devine

thought of a certain young lady with a brown, peach-like complexion, he had serious misgivings as to their future journeyings.

The girl in the meantime, full of various emotions, and with the prescience of coming evil heavy upon her, walked rapidly towards the house without daring to turn round and wave a last adieu to her disconsolate lover, for striding up and down the verandah she caught glimpses of her father's form. Koorabyn was a fine house of its kind, though built of wood and only one storey high. Yet the wood was fashioned into gables and quaint designs, and over all, the roses, grapes, and Virginia creeper grew, making it a veritable fairy bower. The rooms were all large and airy and the furniture of becoming dignity, Mr. Franklin being one who had lived in style in England (as his neighbours said) and had transplanted into the wilds of Australia a little of his English taste. Of course, everyone knew that his wife was an Australian, and the daughter of old Wells, the Government contractor —the man who at one time could dictate terms to his employers (we wonder why?) and who had amassed a huge fortune and then turned bankrupt. It is true he saved enough out of his bankruptcy to live comfortably "ever after"—it is a way big bankrupts have! —but after her first dowry of £20,000 no more of her father's money found its way into his daughter's pockets, or rather, into those of her husband, for that gentleman was considerate enough to relieve her of all embarrassment concerning the disposal of so much wealth. We have said that Mr. Franklin had been accustomed to "style" in England, and there was no doubt about it. Anyone could see that by his swagger, for people who have never lived in style never swagger! They don't know how. There are many who consider such a thing vulgar. Well, that is a mere matter of opinion. All fairly-educated young Englishmen who go to Australia know its value. Ask them. You see, they do not swagger in Australia, they can't—it is not in their nature. An Australian swaggering is like an elephant dancing —he is ungainly. But an Englishman swaggers naturally, as though he had done nothing but swagger from the day of his birth. At home he may be nothing but a City clerk, or, perhaps, the languid son of a West End tradesman. If so, he swaggers more than ever when he sets foot on a shore which can boast of nothing better than a host of vulgar knights. Pah! People at home turn up their noses at a knighthood!

Now it is a peculiarity of human nature that it will yearn for that which it does not possess, and for a trifle light as air it will throw aside the most solid advantages. But the trifle must glitter if it would attract a woman; must fascinate if it would sway a

man. Now, in Australia, the best English manu-
factured swagger is always at a premium, because,
you see, it is a thing which no colonial manufacturer
can turn out, and, as it is much sought after by a certain fair section of the colonists, its price, like that of
diamonds or any other jewel affected by ladies, is
always high.   It is true the colonial men do not set
the same value on it, but as it is a thing they do not
understand, their non-appreciation of it is only natural
—they are so uncouth!   The colonial girl who
breathes the exalted air of the Australian upper
circles looks down upon them with a lofty disdain, so
lofty, indeed, that one wonders if she ever had a
brother.

Miss Wells was such a girl as this.   She thoroughly
despised her own countrymen, and could not see that
though they were a bit rough and blunt on the sur-
face, it was but the breeze that flutters the face of
the ocean ; beneath, they were firm, self-reliant, capable
of great deeds and great love.   But of what use are
such qualities when hidden ?   They want bringing
forth, and good women only can do it.   She didn't
doubt that her countrymen were honourable enough,
and capable, with opportunity, of a good deal ; but
there was no denying that they had not the stamp of
Vere de Vere ; indeed, they had hardly shaken the
mud of the diggings from their boots !

Now, in the exclusive set to which she belonged,

D

and of which she was so bright an ornament, the English visitor of note, and of no note, was invariably received, and, providing he had plenty of style, was usually considered a valuable acquisition, and his chances of catching an heiress were exceedingly rosy; though, were he void of swagger, his chances faded off to zero. As well marry a colonial at once! It was thus the fastidious Miss Wells met Mr. Charles Franklin, a lieutenant in the Dragoon Guards, then on "leave," and her fate was sealed. There was no denying Mr. Franklin's style; it was exquisite— simply ravishing. At least it ravished her of her heart and fortune, and when he led her to the altar he congratulated himself on the success of his undertaking, for everyone knew her father was rolling in money, and that she was the only child. He had only spent three months in the d——d country, so he wrote to a friend, but he had hooked a good thing, and he supposed he would have to settle down there as the affair (what "affair," we wonder? So many swaggerers leave little affairs unsettled in the Old Country!) would take some time to blow over. He hated the d——d colonials, but added that their money was evidently negotiable, and he must be content to remain an exile till the old man (meaning her father), who was beastly rich, went under.

They began their married life by purchasing the

station of Koorabyn, never a very profitable concern, though this fact was skilfully hidden from them, and the ex-dragoon turned squatter, thinking that would prove the nearest approach to a nobleman's life in England. For a little while he was rather amused with the novelty of the life, but once its newness wore off he thought that penal servitude was preferable, and yearned to clutch his father-in-law's fabulous money-bags. Of course there was Melbourne. There one could occasionally get a glimpse of civilisation, a bad one to be sure, yet still a glimpse ; and to Melbourne he accordingly journeyed oftener than became one who had his subsistence to gain from the soil. It was then his wife discovered that a man of good manners is not necessarily a good man. Indeed, it is mostly the other way about, though we all make a virtue of our fancy. In his case all that had most attracted her ignorant imagination proved to be but the thinnest of veneer, which three months of married life had worn off in sundry places. If great Nature must change, why not all things ? He was no worse than the rest of his kind—vain, impudent, selfish. There are thousands such. Had she been an English girl she would have taken him at a different valuation. As it was she ran his stock up to a ridiculous price. It was sure to fall ; it is the nature of such things. Nevertheless, it would be putting it mildly to say that she was disappointed. She strove, as only a woman

D 2

can, to believe in her ideal, to still keep him on his
pedestal above all other men, though she knew his
face was brass and his feet of clay. But now his
every action dispelled the fond illusion, and the voice
which had once so charmed her rang strangely,
almost irritatingly, in her ears. This is one of
the saddest things which can befall a husband
or wife. Woe be unto that household in which the
spirit of irritation enters. It looks a little thing at
first, but, upas-like, it will spread, warping as it
marches.

It may be doubted if the most charming-mannered
men make the best of husbands, for to be charming
one must expend a considerable amount of art (man
not being naturally charming), and when one is always
acting, one instinctively becomes an actor—artificial
—the opposite of the real. If you had been pre-
sumptuous enough to ask Mrs. Franklin if she were
happy, she would have told you decidedly, yes—that
is, if she had condescended to answer you—and she
might have smiled, too, though, had you noticed the
corners of her mouth, you might have seen them curl
into a little quiver. She, however, was not destined for
the *rôle* of martyr. At the birth of her first child
(whom we have already seen grown to lovely womanhood) she suffered more than should fall to the lot
of woman, and at the birth of her second (which was
still-born) she died.

It is only just to say that Mr. Franklin was exceedingly cut up at this calamity, and about three weeks after the sad event he took his little daughter with him to Melbourne, leaving the station in charge of a worthless and profligate overseer. In the capital he put the child to school, and then sought "surcease of sorrow" with a few bachelor acquaintances— much to the disgust of the old Government contractor (who had not yet turned bankrupt). He sent for him one day, gave him a "piece of his mind," and then shut the door upon him. Thus was it that Mr. Franklin began his downward course, and in the Billabong district it was known that Koorabyn was barely self-supporting, while it was suspected, and even whispered, that its owner was in arrears.

This, then, was the gentleman whom Alice beheld perambulating the verandah with a perverse look upon his face. The roses, honeysuckle, and lilac might bloom and perfume, turning the house into another Titania's bower, for aught he cared. When one has to deal with unpleasant things one sees small glory in the sun, and none at all in the stars; and when you see that haunted-looking woman with the pale, terrified face staring moodily into the insidious river, you may wager your salvation that she is not contemplating the sighing, restless water with a rapt, poetic soul, though who knows but that she may form the subject of a poem too—another "Bridge of Sighs."

When Alice stepped on to the verandah her father ceased his rapid stride and turned to her a ruffled countenance. There were yet, it is true, some traces of that beauty which had captivated her mother, though dissipation and disappointment had hardened the mouth and turned the beautiful blue English eyes—those eyes which had seemed to Mrs. Franklin like bits of the bluest heaven—into the strangest study of red and yellow. They looked weak too —a not uncommon failing with blue eyes at a certain age—and had their owner been a play-actor he would have found no difficulty in moving himself to tears, if he could not have moved his audience.

"Ah !" he cried, as he beheld his daughter, "there you are ! " He advanced towards her as he spoke and peered closely into her face. She retreated back amongst the honeysuckle, which at once seized the opportunity of framing her, as it were, with beauty. He saw it, and a quick, eager light beamed from his unpleasant eyes—for his eyes were unpleasant, and it is useless to pretend they were not. We are sorry that the father of our heroine should have even this trifling fault, but truth is great and shall prevail.

"Yes," he continued, as if speaking to himself,

"you are pretty, by Jove! Exactly like your mother —poor mother!" People in misfortune always think, or try to think, well of those whom they have wronged, which shows that deep down the human heart is still distinctly noble! "You ought to have had my eyes though," he went on, "my eyes as they were, not as they are now. Set in that dark face of yours, you would have been simply irresistible. Talk about Helen or Cleopatra, or that hussy for whom Alexander set a town on fire; why, my dear, they wouldn't have been in it with you."

The girl smiled oddly, for it was not often her father held forth in this enthusiastic manner. She, however, knew him well enough to guess some motive for this praise, and had she not known of his indebtedness to Mr. Wingrove she would still have understood, and valued his admiration according to that knowledge.

"Thank you, papa," she replied, "but I am quite satisfied with my eyes as they are; though I have no doubt that the contrast of the blue and the brown would be most striking."

"Striking," exclaimed her father, "it is wonderful! I knew a lady once with such a pair of eyes (she was a colonial too—I wonder where she got them!)—eyes that shone out from her brown face like two great stars. By heaven, I've seen some faces and I've seen some eyes—for we have both in England, faces that are faces and eyes that are eyes; not your dried-up colonial make-believes—but none of them ever equalled hers."

"Mamma's eyes were brown," said the girl.

"I believe they were, my dear. Yes, brown," he added quickly, "brown and beautiful—just like yours."

"Then you think any eyes may be beautiful?"

"In your face, yes." He stooped and kissed her as he spoke.

"So," thought she, "these must have been the sort of speeches with which he won poor mamma, and he means them just as little." This unnatural and undutiful thought was owing to her grandfather's training, for that old gentleman, before he died, had taken her under his protection for a time, and had failed to instil into her that reverence for the parent which every well-regulated child should feel.

"By the way," said Mr. Franklin suddenly, "if you had come in ten minutes sooner you would have met a very distinguished visitor."

"Indeed." The girl immediately began to freeze. The word came like a breath from the South Pole. Stanford, Wingrove—all that she had heard flashed through her mind in a moment. She did not think it necessary to ask the visitor's name.

" You are not very curious, my daughter. An un-natural trait in a woman."

" Am I not ? "

" It might have been the Governor."

" But he is not a very distinguished man."

" They never are—for if they were they would not be colonial Governors. Colonial Governor!" he re-peated disdainfully. " Why, it sounds almost as bad as colonial bishop! "

" We will dispense with both in good time."

" Throw off the British yoke, eh, my little Repub-lican ? " he laughed. " Never, my dear, never while there are knighthoods to be given away."

" Ah," she cried with a glow of patriotism, " wait till we get rid of all the old colonists; wait till Australian men govern Australia, then we shall see."

" The old colonists are the prop and mainstay of the country ; your young colonial is only fit——And yet," he added changing his tone with significant haste, " I daresay some of the coming colonials "—he never by any chance called them Australians, that being too dignified and national a word—" are very good men in their way. There is, after all, little in common between the man whose sympathies are all with the Old Country and the native whose sym-pathies are all with this. You see, the former cannot shake off his old prejudices and the latter cannot understand them. One of the two must go to the wall, and youth will tell."

"And has it taken you twenty years to discover that, papa?"

"It takes most men a lifetime to rid themselves of a superstition. I must confess that I had formed a not very flattering estimate of colonial ability; yet, since I have become intimate with my neighbour Wingrove, my impressions have undergone a considerable change."

So, it was coming, but she was prepared. Her lips went closer together and she began to tremble just a little.

"Mr. Wingrove is hardly the sort of man I should have thought capable of working so great a change. I thought you so thoroughly detested all things colonial that no earthly power could change you."

"Wingrove is a very intelligent man, my dear, and —for a colonial—a deuced decent fellow. Not English, of course; one does not expect that. But he's not half bad, and, besides, he has a future. He will most certainly be the next Premier."

"No doubt he is worthy of the office."

"Well, I don't think much of the office myself," said her father patronisingly; "it's not like the English office, you know; but if he toadies enough he's almost sure of a knighthood. We don't think much of knights at home, but here in a would-be

republican country it's different. However, knighthood, or no knighthood, Wingrove is a very able
man."

"I am glad you think so, papa."

"Don't you?"

"I do not, and what is more, I do not like the
man."

"That's a misfortune, my dear, a very great misfortune, for he is a profound admirer of yours."

"How can you, papa?"

"Why, my dear, what do you mean? Wingrove
is an honourable man, and I consider he has honoured
you greatly."

"How honoured me?" asked the girl with a
quivering voice.

"My dear," said her father suddenly, taking her
hand and smoothing it in an affectionate manner,
"have you never thought of the time that is to come
when I shall no longer be able to work for you?
Have you never thought that at any day, any hour I
may be taken from you?" The girl hung her head
trembling, but answered not. "I see you have not,"
he went on, "it is so like a child. But to me my
first duty has ever been the protection of those I love.
I have long known of Wingrove's affection, adoration—for so I must call it—and to-day he has
honoured us by offering you marriage." There was
an unusual quiver in her father's voice as he spoke

these words, and he had to turn away from her imploring eyes.

"Honour us! Marry me! What do you mean?"

He was silent a moment, though he still held her hand, and she felt a shiver run through his fingers. It was but a momentary struggle, however. He turned his eyes to her and they looked harder and more unpleasant than ever.

"Yes," he said coldly, "he has offered you marriage, and I am very sensible of the honour he would confer upon us. It is but right and proper that you should marry now, and as he is rich and powerful, and will most certainly have a future, I really don't see that you could do better. He may, upon occasion, be a trifle rough, but he doesn't drop his h's; and, my dear," he added, as if what he was about to say were reason enough in itself, "no girl should remain single after twenty."

The girl withdrew her hand from his with a gesture of pain. "I am sorry, papa, but I do not care for Mr. Wingrove."

"My dear," he said with a smile, charmed completely with her innocence, "no one wants you to. It is not a matter of caring; it is a matter of diplomacy."

"But I would not marry a man I did not love."

"Arcadian argument, my dear. Marriage is simply a matter of interest. Love matches, and such-like

stuff, are only found in books, and then they leave off
with the sound of the wedding bells because the
author dare not go on with the sequel. Come now,
you are a sensible girl. What shall I say to Mr.
Wingrove when he calls?"

"Tell him that I would not marry him if he were
the only man in the world."

"You are a little fool. You don't know what you
are saying."

"Perhaps not."

"No impertinence, Miss. Listen to me. Mr.
Wingrove has been good enough to make this offer,
and you must accept it."

"Must, papa?"

"Yes, *must!*" He seized her arm as he spoke
and scowled fiercely into her face. "It is imperative
—a matter of life and death. There, there, don't ask
me to explain. You will be as happy as the day is
long; you will have no whim, no fancy which that
man will not be able to gratify. He loves you very
dearly—nay, I might say madly, passionately. I am
sure he will make a good husband of whom we shall
both be proud."

"Father," she said—it was not often she called
him by that most dignified of names, and when she
did he knew there was something of importance
coming—"how can you so degrade yourself by
singing the praises of that dreadful man when you

know that every word, every sentiment you utter is false ?"

A fearful oath escaped the guilty man's lips, his eyes shone horribly, and he clenched his fist as though to fell her. It was then she caught a glimpse of that nature which had destroyed her mother's fond ideal.

"How dare you," he gasped, "how dare you ? By heaven, if you were not a girl——"

"Father," she said coldly, never flinching an inch, but returning his furious gaze with a look of unutterable disdain, "what is the use of this pretence, this subterfuge ? Why did you not come to me," she went on half hysterically, "and say, 'I owe Wingrove a sum of money, which I cannot pay. He has seen you, he would like to buy you. Come, let us make a bargain.' It would, at least, have been straightforward, and we should have known on what ground we were standing."

"Well," said he with a cynical laugh, "you are a Tartar; and though I should very much like to beat you, and you deserve it, I must bow to your impertinence. Modesty alone forbade me from being as rude as you propose; but, since you suggest plainspeaking, let us beat no more about the bush. Well then, I do owe Wingrove money—three thousand pounds—which he will willingly forego, and dower you with twenty thousand more, if you will marry him. It is a large sum." She remained silent. Now her passion had flown she was only a poor, weak little woman, who would have given the world to have been able to hide herself away, and cry to her heart's content. "A very large sum," he continued, "and one not to be picked up every day. Your dower will ensure your future; the removal of the mortgage from my estate will make me a happy man. You see, the future is entirely in your hands. You may make or mar us. It is for you to say whether we shall live or die." He laughed in the same cynical way, and lit a cigarette, watching her closely as he did so. "Oh, by the way," he added after a moment's silence, "where did you get your information?"

"From Mr. Stanford."

"Am I right then in supposing that he has presumed to approach you with any of his nonsense?"

She grew crimson, even to her neck, and falling on her knees before him burst into tears.

"Ah," said he, "this is more serious than I imagined."

"Pity me," she cried, "I am not undutiful, indeed I am not."

"Your actions shall prove the truth of your assertion. But come, come, my child," he added tenderly, stroking her hair gently as he spoke, "this is a free country, the freest of all free countries—any colonial will tell you that! You are your own mistress, and may do whatsoever you please. All I would have you recollect is that I am your father, and that I am utterly powerless to ward off disaster except through you. I will not go so far as to say that it is your duty to save me—that is a question between you and your conscience; but remember that I am entirely at your mercy, and that it rests with you whether I live or die."

CHAPTER IV.

THE MEMBER FOR BILLABONG.

MR. MARTIN WINGROVE, of Wingrove Station, Billabong, in the colony of Victoria, was not alone the
most prosperous and wealthy land and stock owner in
the district, but he could also write M.P., J.P., and
several other distinguishing letters after his honoured
patronymic. He was also the chairman of the United
Pastoralists' Union—a vast concern which had its
finger in almost every pastoral pie in the country,
particularly in the Queensland parts. He was also
sole owner of the Great Mount Desolation Gold Mine,
though that of late had proved the least paying of his
many properties. That he was a great man in the
district there was no gainsaying, and people would tell
you that, even in Melbourne, he wielded a monarch's
power, and was received obsequiously by the city's
most influential potentates. And more power to him,
was the cry, for was it not universally known that he
had won his present proud eminence by sheer hard
work, against a thousand natural impediments? No
frank nature could withhold applause from such a
man; Mr. Wingrove was consequently applauded.
The world recognises that there is no real honour in

E

that greatness which is thrust upon a man; the man, too, recognises it; let him win it, though, and like the sun it is a perpetual delight.

It was whispered—for there are always whisperings, and the higher a man rises the louder howl the curs beneath him—it was whispered that Mr. Wingrove's father, Old Jim, as he was familiarly termed in the early days, had come to the country in a Government ship; though whether it was true or not, no one could say. No one would have presumed to hint at such a thing in the presence of so rich a man as Old Jim's son, while Old Jim himself had been dead so many years, that the rising generation knew him not. Yet it is very singular how murder will out, and how people will get hold of your past weaknesses or crimes in spite of the utmost secrecy. The prying propensity of the human being is appalling, and the love to degrade the species one of the most astonishing and undeniable of truths. One little vice will overshadow a thousand virtues; and as the poor on earth look forward to the crown of gold in heaven, and enjoy no small satisfaction from the thought that they shall spend eternity in bliss, while the rich man moans, in unspeakable pain, for a drop of water; so, with a somewhat similar satisfaction, did all who knew him, and envied his prosperity, regard Old Jim. Whereas poverty was no crime, that of transportation left an indelible stain. Yet was he transported? How could they really tell. Had they not burnt the public records in Sydney? Yet fire will not purge all things; oblivion only can annihilate Botany Bay. There is no hope for such a name.

How people had got the idea into their heads that Old Jim had been transported, it would be difficult to say, but it was there nevertheless; and there is a story extant which tells of the arrival at Wingrove Station of a tramp, or sundowner, as they call them, who marched up to Old Jim as he stood among his men and called him by the familiar name of "pal;" and it is also said that Old Jim turned pale beneath his tan, and seizing the fellow's arm hurried him off. But who that swagman was, whence came he or whither he went, no man could tell. There were many, also, who doubted the honest increase of the old man's flocks and herds, but of them we have little to say. Success, if it does not shut uncivil mouths, at least makes people speak between their teeth. When the old man's turn came he died respected and honoured; and his son Martin, who was being educated in Melbourne at the time, stepped into one of the prettiest properties in the country; not rich, but capable of richness; a property with a promise. Martin soon grasped the situation, and being of an enterprising and ambitious nature he quickly rose to an eminence undreamt of by his father. He acquired land in every direction, invested in the newest

E 2

machinery, and being a man of discretion as well as
foresight, soon built himself up a large fortune. Then
he turned his thoughts to politics and contested the
Billabong district, which only returned one member,
and was duly elected. It is quite true that he sank
in the estimation of the Squatocracy over this
business, for what gentleman could possibly mix himself up with colonial politics? To this he replied that
it was time gentlemen did begin to consider politics,
for the cheapjacks, who had so long posed as poli-
ticians, were sending the country to the dogs—an
unanswerable argument. In debate he showed a
certain impudence and obstinacy which soon won for
him universal recognition as the coming man; and
that he hoped to win the highest political office in the
colony there can be no doubt; and that he had every
chance of so doing no one could deny.

Mr. Wingrove was a widower, childless, and at the
time our story opens was in his forty-third year. He
was rather below than above the medium height, yet
broad and sinewy, showing both strength and agility
in his compact figure. His complexion was fair and
freckled, as fair complexions in hot countries often
are; his hair and beard were of a light red colour,
which in some lights looked golden, in others of the
colour of blood. He had a pair of steel-blue eyes, of
a singularly penetrating nature, and a high, benevo-
lent brow, round which the hair had thinned con-

siderably. People would tell you that he was a strange
mixture of good and bad, that he might either perso-
nate the saint or the fury. His voice, too, could be
soft as a woman's when he pleased; though when he
sat in court and sentenced evildoers it might have
been another Rhadamanthus come to judgment. Or
hear his station hands describe him in a rage! They
used to say that his head contracted like a snake's,
that he hissed the words instead of speaking them,
and that his eyes used to burn like white-hot metal.
But then servants, like poets, are " such awful liars,"
and one must take the news of the kitchen or the
yard *cum grano salis*.

It was the morning after Miss Franklin's interview
with her father, and Mr. Wingrove was busily employed, in that large airy room of his which he dignified by the name of study, composing his anticipated
attack on the Government—an attack which was to
demolish his opponents, and place in his hands the reins
of the State—when he heard a timid knock at the
door, for it is no trifling thing to disturb a great man's
meditations. But as he at that moment was making
a most important point in his argument he took no
notice of the sound, and not till it was repeated did he
cry angrily "Come in!" A servant entered timidly.
Miss Franklin had ridden over from Koorabyn.
Would he see her?

"Yes, yes. Show her in by all means."

He sprang to his feet with a triumphant smile, passed his hand through his beard, curled his moustache afresh, and smoothed the hair which he had unconsciously ruffled during the throes of composition. The next moment Miss Franklin entered, looking very pale and excited, but, so the member thought, exceedingly lovely.

"Delighted to see you, Miss Franklin," he said, offering her a chair as he spoke, which she accepted with a slight inclination of the head, "delighted and surprised," he went on, "for it is not often you condescend to honour my house with your presence."

"I have come," she said, waving her hand impatiently, in which she held a little gold-headed riding whip, "I have come, Mr. Wingrove, on a—on a matter of business." She hesitated, then brought out the word with a sudden defiance.

He laughed. "Business! Really, Miss Franklin, don't speak of such a dreadful thing. Surely we can find other and more pleasant topics. I think I could if I tried. But, you will pardon me for saying so, you look far from well." Yet his steely eyes wandered devouringly over her face and figure. He thought the habit clung to her like a glove, and did not wonder at it.

"Oh," she laughed, with just a tinge of bitterness, "I am quite well, thank you."

"I am delighted to hear it. But may I offer you some refreshment ?"

"No, thank you."

"I am sure you must be tired after your long ride," he insisted.

"Not in the least," she answered coldly.

Lounging back in his easy chair, he rested his chin upon his hand and watched her closely.

"Yes," so ran his thoughts, "she is beautiful, the most beautiful of them all. A girl worth fighting for ! A girl in a million." But he said aloud, "I really wish you would permit me to display my hospitality in some form or other."

"Mr. Wingrove," she said. ignoring his remark, and rushing abruptly and blindly to the object of her visit, " can you not guess the reason which brings me here ?" She dropped her eyes as she spoke, blushed, and looked confused.

"If I dared to hope," he replied, "I should say that you had come to thank me for the pony you did me the honour to accept."

"I cannot accept it," she said. " I—I am very sorry, and I thank you ; but father has told me all, and it is better we should understand each other now." Her colour came and went, and she trembled visibly. Yet that spirit which had given her sufficient courage to beard the lion thus, stood her in good stead. She may quiver (for who shall control the blood or nerves?), but her courage and purpose are fixed, unchangeable.

"I am sorry you do not like the pony," was his reply. "I had it broken in especially for you."

"You are very kind," she began.

"It is nothing," he said in a low, meaning voice, "to what I would do if you would only give me the permission."

"It is of that I would speak," she replied in a low voice, the blood rushing furiously to her face. It was no ordinary ordeal this, and she felt her position in all its cruelty ; but the woman who loves can fight, in her own sweet way, as well as the man. "My father has told me of your generous offer, and I am sure I appreciate the honour you would confer upon us ; but —but I know you are too honourable to take any woman who could only give her hand."

"It is for that hand I have asked," he said with a strange smile. "Give it to me. It shall be reverenced like a god."

"I mean," she said, "that I have never thought of you as anything but a friend."

"I see," he laughed ; "you mean you do not love me as a wife should love. I doubt it not ; as yet I am unworthy of you. But," he added, rising—his voice now earnest and full of meaning—"I love you, love you with all my soul, and my love is great enough to kindle even your indifference. Marry me, and I swear to you that you shall never repent it. You shall be your own mistress in everything. I will never cross your purpose with so much as a single word. I will guard you as man has never guarded woman. I will love you as woman was never loved before. My wealth, my life itself, shall be at your disposal." He paced before her excitedly as he spoke, occasionally stopping to emphasise a word, an action.

She shrank back terrified at the vehemence of his passion, but answered in a low voice, " I am sorry, so sorry, but I never dreamt of this."

" Of course not," he replied with a savage laugh—feeling half angry with himself at this confession of weakness—" that is the way with you women. You break a man's heart and then tell him you never meant to. Do you then think that men are mere blocks of wood without soul or feeling ? "

" But never by word or action," said she, looking up with sudden determination, "have I given you to understand that I regarded you as anything but a friend."

He laughed harshly. " Why do you trifle with me ? How could I be your friend when to see you is to love you ? Do you never look in your glass ? Don't you know that the very sight of you is enough to set a man's heart beating ? that the mere idea of your presence is an intoxicant ? Listen to me," he went on, drawing still closer to her, " I love you, I love you, for good or evil, for better or worse. If I spoke for a thousand years I could not say more than that, I could not mean more. I love you."

She arose with a look of terror on her face. "You must not speak like this. I cannot listen to you."

"Why are you here then—to taunt me, to drive me mad?"

"I came," she said, speaking painfully, "to appeal to your honour and your better nature; to tell you that however much I may feel flattered and honoured by your condescension, I cannot accept your offer because—oh, because I—I do not love you."

"I have told you," he replied, "that I love you. I will leave the rest to fate." She made no answer, but with a despairing gesture hid her face in her hands. "It cannot be," he continued after a brief pause, and his eyes gleamed strangely as he put the question, "it cannot be that you are shackled in any way—that your affections are given to another?"

"Yes," she said, turning her dauntless eyes full upon him, as though the thought had given her courage, "I do love another."

"I imagined as much," he sneered: "your father's servant! And do you think your father will permit such a *mésalliance?* He is discharged, I believe. He will quit the district. You will forget that you were once foolish. Come, come. Think over what I have said. I neither press nor force you against your will.

You must come to me of your own free choice and offer me your wifely allegiance. That is all I ask. In return you shall have a life's devotion and all that wealth can procure. Your father favours my suit. That, at least, should have some weight with a daughter's decision. I will not say what I can do for you, for I could not do too much; but I will leave your own good sense to distinguish the wisest policy, and to foresee the numerous benefits which would accrue to you and yours from such a marriage." He paused, surveying her for a moment, then added quickly, "You will understand, Miss Franklin, that these things are a mere secondary consideration, and should receive no mention from me in an affair of this nature had I not wished to prove how sincere my admiration is, and how I would, by many a little act, try to repay you for the inestimable blessing you had conferred upon me by giving me yourself."

Her lips curled in a disdainful little smile. "And should I not confer that inestimable blessing?"

"Pray do not even hint at so overwhelming a thought."

She tried to say hard, cruel things, but could not. So her mission had ended thus. She had come here with the intention of falling at his feet and imploring him to spare her and her father; to give them time and they would pay off the mortgage. She would appeal to his better nature; humiliate herself before

him. What mattered it so that she gained her end ?
A thousand sympathetic speeches she composed
during that long, long night ; yet she had no sooner
entered his presence than all her humility fled ; the
spirit of antagonism rose strong within her; she
could not stoop. Indeed, had it not been for her
father's sake she would have listened to no word of
his passion, for every syllable he uttered cut her like
a knife. Yet, thanks to that father's training, she
could at times be diplomatic before aught else, and
she treated him with all the courtesy her outraged
feelings would permit. And was the visit to end in
nothing ? She hoped not once ; she feared not now.
She had heard a declaration so passionate that she
trembled at the recollection, intuitively guessing that
henceforth there was to be no peace for her. It is
true he had only hinted at her father's obligations, and
had treated her with a courtliness she had little expected; but her woman's heart mistrusted him all the
same, and whenever she looked into his strange eyes,
which seemed in his more passionate moments to burn
white, she felt a terror and loathing rise against him.
Still she must smile as best she may, and, as her
father would say, be a diplomatist before aught else.
Who shall say what the morrow may bring forth ?

He showed her to the door, out through the hall,
and helped her to mount her horse. He pressed her
little hand significantly as he said good-bye.

"Pity me, Alice," he whispered in a passionate undertone, " for God's sake pity me ! "

She cast a sudden look at him, but he was leaning over her hand, which he reverentially carried to his lips. Then with a low bow he stood back, and the great horse, tossing its head in the air, darted off like a swallow.

Mr. Wingrove stood watching her till a bend in the road hid her flying form, and then with a look of the most intense satisfaction he retraced his steps to the study. Once there he paced the room restlessly for fully half an hour, talking and gesticulating in a manner most unusual with him. He pictured innumerable scenes, held innumerable imaginary conversations. Now was his voice soft and tender, as it had been a short time ago when he declared the depth of his affection; now was it shrill and fierce— for he no longer spoke with her, but with him—with him who had come between them. Then was it his eyes glowed with a white heat, while little red sparks shot, or seemed to shoot, from them, as they will from steel when heated white. He clenched his hands and dug his heels savagely into the carpet as he walked, stopping now and again to utter some fiercer threat, to deliver an oath with surpassing emphasis.

" She loves him," he muttered, grinding the words between his teeth as though he would like to rend them ; " loves him, and has the audacity to tell me so.

Well, so much the better, so much greater the triumph, for she shall be mine in spite of them all! Mine, mine," he went on almost savagely.   " Yes, all mine! You are mine!" He held out his arms as he spoke, as though embracing the object of his thoughts. " I hold you to me, I press you till you faint; I kiss your mouth, your eyes, your hair, for you are mine, and I shall kiss you till we die!   Bah!" he exclaimed with sudden fervour, flinging open his arms as though to release his imaginary mistress, " what a fool I am."

He wiped his brow, for so real had been his imaginings that the sweat stood out upon it in great glistening drops, while he panted like one who has experienced a real excitement. He poured himself out a long draught of wine and quaffed it eagerly; then recommenced his wanderings up and down the carpet, but no longer with an eager step, for his passion had spent its force, and he was, to all outward appearance, composed, serene.   Presently he sat himself at his desk and began once more the composition of his attack on the Government, but after a few moments' reflection he was again disturbed by another knock at the door.

" Come in!" he cried brusquely, for he whom we have but lately seen in soft conversation with Miss Franklin was a different being from the Mr. Wingrove of Billabong; " come in!"

The words had scarcely left his lips when the door swung suddenly open, and, to his surprise and annoyance, in stalked Mr. Thomas Stanford.

"Well, sir," thundered the Member, bounding angrily to his feet, "what brings you here?"

"You." It is painfully evident that Mr. Thomas Stanford is as rash and undiplomatic as his sweetheart.

"Indeed. I am sure the business which brings you here must be of a very important nature."

"It is."

"Will you be seated?"

"No, thank you; what I have to say can be said standing."

"Very well." Mr. Wingrove smiled and resumed his seat.

"You have," began Stanford in a low, clear tone, "you have lately been honoured with a certain lady's presence—pray keep your seat, sir," as Wingrove rose with an oath—"there is no necessity to mention names. I think we understand each other."

"Has the lady been good enough to appoint you her champion? Has she conveyed to you the gist of our interview?"

"The lady is entirely ignorant of my visit, and I have appointed myself her champion."

"Very interesting, no doubt," said the Member with a sneer, "if one could comprehend it. But is

this all the business you have come upon, because, if
it is, I would beg to remind you that I am a busy
man, Mr.—Mr.—what is your name?"

Tom smiled grimly.   "Stanford," he said; "your
father would have remembered it better."

There was something in this speech, a sort of
covert meaning, which made Mr. Wingrove burn.
His thoughts flew instantly back to a certain
Captain Stanford, who at one time had been connected with the police, but, being a wise man, he
pressed for no explanation.

"Well, Mr. Stanford," he said, "what is the object
of your visit?"

"I have come to ask you a favour."

"Your confidence is assuring; but I am not aware
that you have any call on my consideration."

"Perhaps not.   But I may be a firm believer in
your charity."

Wingrove looked at him and smiled, though his
eyes began to shift uneasily.   There was something
lying behind all this, though Stanford's face was
Sphinx-like, impenetrable.

"Well, well?" he asked somewhat testily.

Stanford curled his moustache before replying.

"I am aware, as you phrase it, that I have no call
upon your consideration, but I may have great hopes
from your sense of justice, and when you know all
your honour will, I am sure, forbid you to go a step

further in this matter. You asked me just now
had that lady appointed me her champion, and I
replied, no; but, nevertheless, I am her champion by
all that men and heaven hold sacred."

"You are married, then?"

"No"—Wingrove breathed freely—"but we are
betrothed."

"Indeed! and what has all this to do with
me?"

"This: that now I have spoken you will understand that lady's position, and respect it accordingly."

"Let me tell you," said Wingrove, rising, the
anger almost bursting the swollen veins on his forehead, "that I allow no man to dictate to me in any
way whatever. That is my answer; now withdraw.
The next time you venture here on such a mission
you shall be received in a fitting manner. Go!"

"Listen to me, Martin Wingrove. Annoy that
lady in any way and I will whip you within an inch
of your life."

With a great oath the Member sprang towards
him, but quick as lightning Stanford's hands went
up. The Member drew back. An encounter with
that tall, fierce man might be fraught with no little
personal injury.

"I threatened to do it once," he continued; "it
will be no vain threat the next time. I will not have
you approach that lady except by way of gratitude

F

for the honour she confers upon you by admitting you into her presence."

"Look you, Mr. Stanford," said the Member, clutching nervously at the back of his chair, his face ghastly white with rage, his whole body denoting the fierce excitement under which he laboured, "you shall regret these words of yours to the last moment of your life ; you will curse your foolhardiness every day till you die, and on your dying bed—if you ever die in one—you will wish your tongue had rotted to the roots before you had made an enemy of me."

Stanford's eyes flashed ominously. " Why, you dog," he said, " I would thrash you now if it were not for the taint of Botany Bay that clings to you."

The Member grew livid to the lips, and had it not been for the support of his chair might have tottered to the ground. He tried to speak, but the words bubbled from his lips in unintelligible sound. He waved his hand with an impatient gesture.

" Go, go !" he hissed as soon as he regained command of his tongue, " go, and think yourself lucky that I don't order my men to whip you from the place. I had hitherto regarded you with pity, as we do the worm when we crush it; but now I know you to be a reptile in my path, I will set my foot on your head, I will grind you in the dust."

Stanford laughed. " You will do exactly all the harm that you are able, not all that you would do.

But remember one thing, Martin Wingrove, that though you were as rich as you are vindictive, your wealth shall avail you nothing against my vengeance."

" We shall see."

" Yes, we shall see."

" Yes," repeated Wingrove, as he paced his room alone, his livid face and white-hot eyes telling more plainly than words the fury of the storm within, " we shall see, we shall see."

CHAPTER V.

THE MEMBER SPEAKS.

IT was a week after the events related in the preceding chapter, and during the whole of that time the two rivals had left the object of their rivalry, as far as they were concerned, in sorrowful seclusion. Wingrove spent not a little of that period in his study, composing his great attack on the Government. Incidents of late had contrived to render him so bitter towards all things human that he fairly thrilled as he indited the burning words, and he looked forward with intense satisfaction to the effect of that speech upon the country. But there were other things that interested him equally, perhaps more than the composition of his philippic ; and from the contemplation of them he became inspired with that divine fury which was to wither his political opponents. But in his calmer, saner moments he thought it would be more becoming his dignity if he abandoned all thoughts of the wilful girl—went near Koorabyn no more. Was he to bow, and whine, and scrape—he, the richest man in the district !—for the sake of one who had no spark of affection for him—he, who by holding out his arms might beckon the loveliest to

him? Faith, not he! It was undignified, un-
becoming. He would have no more of it; nor would
he, had there been no other thought to trample upon
his good resolutions. He could sacrifice much, dare
much, but he could not leave the field to his rival.
To part with her was one thing, to hand her over to
him was another.

He brooded over this thought as he sat at meals,
as he rode, walked, wrote; he dreamt of it by night.
It divided, nay, seemed to threaten, a monopoly of his
attention. He struggled with it valiantly, vainly, for
six days; on the seventh he mounted his big black
horse and galloped over to Koorabyn.

Mr. Franklin had espied him coming along the
road, so that when the great man, after dismounting
and making his horse fast to a rail (for in the Australian bush people are taught to look after themselves), walked up the little private path that led to
the front entrance, he discovered his dear friend
Franklin standing upon the verandah steps, hand
outstretched and a smile of welcome on his face.

"Thought we were never going to see you again,"
said the master of Koorabyn as he shook hands with
his visitor. "Wondered what had become of you all
this time. Thought you must have sneaked off to
Melbourne without giving us warning. Glad to see
you, though; come in and have a drink."

"Thank you, I will. The road was a bit dusty."

Mr. Franklin led his guest through the long hall, or, as it was more commonly called, the passage, to a cosy little room at the back of the house which he dignified by the name of study. A couch, a couple of easy chairs; a square mahogany table in one corner, a bookshelf in the other; a gun here, a fishing rod there, and some highly coloured sporting prints on the walls comprised the furniture and decorations of this abode of thought. There was a fine plush rack over the mantelpiece, evidently a woman's gift, with a miscellaneous array of pipes in it, from the common clay to the more aristocratic amber-tipped briar; a tobacco jar and cigar box ranged themselves side by side on the afore-mentioned mantelpiece, while on a substantial shelf in one corner were displayed some half-dozen bottles of a suspicious character.

Mr. Wingrove looked round the room with a somewhat critical cast of countenance.

" You seem pretty comfortable here," he said.

" Yes," replied his host as he proceeded to measure out the whisky—for of that precious fluid will the squatter as well as his *employé* drink more than is good for him—" pretty comfortable. You see, it's the only room I can really call my own. Allie runs the rest of the house, and has as great a mania for tidiness as her poor mother had. But here I am monarch of all I survey. If I throw off my boots in that corner, they'll remain there till I come and pick them up.

And if I want to refresh the inner man I can come here and do it without the whole household thinking I am going to the dogs. But here's to you, Wingrove. Glad to see you looking so well."

Now it is decidedly embarrassing to sit at a man's table, so to speak, drink his whisky and soda—good home-made soda too—and hear him straining every effort to please, when you know that he is only thinking of the debt he owes you and wondering if you are going to "cut up rough." But it is still more painful to drink that whisky and listen to his strained advances while you are contemplating him an irreparable injury. It is awkward for both parties; intuition being keen in man. If you are a person of ideas, and used to little difficulties, like Mr. Franklin, you will bear the infliction with an heroic countenance and a fund of inspired commonplace; but if you are a man of one fixed idea, and have no agreeable chatter at your command, like Mr. Wingrove, you will sit scowling in a grim sort of silence and despise the airy nothings you cannot imitate. Now, if Mr. Franklin had not owed Mr. Wingrove a considerable sum of money, it is a thousand to one that the worthy squatter would have considered the Englishman an exceedingly entertaining fellow; but then, you see, he *did* owe him money, and something more, and that simple fact rose before the squatter's mental vision like a huge ghost, and cast a shadow on his host's amiability. The host, on the other hand, knowing how feeble he was in the grasp of his taciturn guest, must needs force the conversation to prevent it flagging. Now as he, at the same time, was cursing his fate beneath his breath, it may not seem surprising that Mr. Wingrove failed to catch the ring of truth in his tones. Therefore the squatter, who had never been accused of weakness, sipped his whisky with evident appreciation, but remained fixed in his purpose; while his host, who had exhausted every effort in his endeavours to ward off what he knew was coming, sank back in his chair and pulled assiduously at his pipe.

"So you are going down for the opening of Parliament, eh?"

"Yes," said Wingrove.

"That will be soon now, will it not?"

"A fortnight." Mr. Wingrove was evidently saving his breath.

"Well," said Mr. Franklin affably, "I suppose there's a good deal in politics when you understand them, but, you know, it must be a deuce of a bother to have to wade through Parliamentary blue-books and statistics."

"It is," said the Member grimly—with just the shade of a sneer.

"And then the piles of Hansards. Good heavens, Wingrove, is any man supposed to read that mountain of rubbish?"

"You're not flattering, Franklin."

"By Jove, pardon me, old fellow. I forgot your speeches were there. I thought it was all colonial rubbish, you know."

"I know," answered Wingrove tartly. "You Englishmen are all alike. Nothing good can grow out of England. And twenty years of residence here has not taught you better. Why, you ought to be a thorough-going colonial by this time, heart and soul."

"About that you must allow me to hold a different opinion. If there is one thing above all others for which I thank God, it is that I was born an Englishman."

"I cannot understand why you should have left such a wonderful place."

Mr. Franklin flushed hotly. There was something horribly insinuating in the Member's voice. Could he have heard of "that affair?" A taunt, another question, rose to his lips, but with an effort he suppressed it. If those words had escaped him it would have gone ill with him at that moment. The question referred to a Government passage, a pestilential phrase—to Wingrove.

"Well," laughed Mr. Franklin, changing with admirable *sang-froid* the unpleasant topic, "it is quite proper and patriotic of you to uphold your country. 'Advance Australia!' is a grand motto, and so that you advance in the right direction you will, I daresay, do something in time. But you shouldn't try to belittle England."

"Nor should Englishmen think they advance her prestige by belittling us. But there, why should we talk? You may taunt and despise us if you think fit; we shall love you none the better for it. But I came here on another and more important business, and I want to know, Franklin, what I am to expect, and how we stand."

So, it had come. The glib chatter had but staved off the inevitable for a time. The cloud was about to burst, and he had neither umbrella nor great-coat.

"You see," continued Wingrove in a cold, dry tone, " I am going down to town in a week's time, and as I shall be away for at least six months——"

"I understand."

" Of course you know I am devotedly attached to Miss Franklin, and that I think the honour she would confer upon me of the most exalted nature ; but will she confer that honour, Franklin, and what am I to do? A man cannot live on air, can he—he cannot go on loving a shadow?"

" No," said Mr. Franklin, "decidedly he cannot."

" Then what hope have I of ultimate success?"

" I have every reason to believe that she is not unfavourable to your suit."

The squatter laughed rather unpleasantly. " Have you? I should have thought it was the other way about. And yet, Franklin, I flatter myself that I am one of whom no woman could be ashamed, and of whom many might be proud."

"There is no doubt of it," was the reply—for what other reply was there? "As I told Alice myself, you are the Coming Man, Wingrove, and your country will be proud of you yet—that is, if it will ever take a pride in anything intellectual." He could not help having his fling at the place even though he knew it angered the man whom he was so eager to please.

"About that," said the Member, ignoring his concluding remark, "my modesty forbids me to speak; but I have always thought that any gentleman was good enough for any lady, and that he even became a most desirable connection when he could write big cheques—and get them honoured too."

"No doubt, no doubt—a most desirable connection. But you have forgotten to take into consideration a young girl's whims and fancies."

"I have lands, position, money," continued Wingrove modestly; "a boundless ambition. I love her; her every wish shall be gratified; she shall have twenty thousand pounds in her own name; she shall be—by heaven, she shall be the first lady in the land!"

"You are a splendid fellow, by jingo!" cried his listener, the thought of so much money moving him to the quick. "The girl must be mad, stark mad."

"Not at all. She is in love."

Mr. Franklin bounded indignantly to his feet. "In love is she, by George! If I thought—but no, Wingrove, you are jesting?"

"Perhaps so"; a queer light shone in the squatter's eyes as he spoke. Mr. Franklin felt it pierce him to the heart.

"Who—who can it be?" he asked.

"Mr. Stanford. But remember, Franklin, he and I are mortal enemies. He must never see her; she must hold neither speech nor correspondence with him. I wish to make her my wife, and with your aid I will."

"My aid? But, my dear sir, I cannot make her marry you."

"You can try. It will be worth your while."

Mr. Franklin bowed his head. It was no use going further into the matter. He understood the squatter's words to mean that through his child alone could he expect salvation; the squatter meant that he should read them in that way. It was terrible, though, to think that his independence, his life, one might say, was in the power of this man. Oh, could he but arise, repay this upstart with the just scorn that was in him, it would have been well; but he felt he dare not move lest the iron hand was clapped upon his shoulder, and the iron voice cried, "Go forth!"

Mr. Wingrove arose with the intention of returning home. He had stated his case, had done a good day's work. There could be no mistake now, if language has any significance. He had treated his victim with the utmost courtesy; but he was determined all the same. He knew that Franklin clung to Koorabyn with all his soul, poor and profitless though it was; he knew that parting from it would prove a death-blow, the wreck of his life. If he knew human nature, the nature of father and daughter, there would be no parting.

"Well, Franklin," he said, "you'll talk it over, won't you? No hurry, you know. I shall be going to town in a week's time. I'll look in again before I go."

Mr. Franklin could have dashed his fist into that impertinent face. There was a tone of victory, of possession in the man's voice that made his blood burn.

"In a week, then, be it."

The Member shook hands cordially, for winners are ever magnanimous, and turned to go, when the strains of a piano reached his ears. He stood still and listened.

"Alice?" he asked.

"Yes."

All unconscious of their presence in the study, she had seated herself at the piano and was now playing some of her dreamiest and saddest music. Wingrove stole softly back to his chair, and sinking into it listened with a wondering look upon his face. His

companion sat forward, his unpleasant eyes absolutely
sparkling with pleasure. There could be no doubt
of one thing: Mr. Franklin thoroughly appreciated
his daughter's playing.

"She will sing in a minute," he whispered; "she
sings like an angel."

The sad strains ceased for a moment, and it
seemed as though the very air stood still to listen—
so marvellously quiet was everything. Then the piano
shrieked suddenly out in a loud, discordant way as
though it were some pain-stricken beast; her fingers
fell swift and strong upon its ivory keys; the whole
house seemed to vibrate; the air was filled with a
thousand strange sounds—the tramp of armies, the
shrieks of the wounded, the sighs of the dying. Mr.
Franklin sat forward with an eager look on his
face; the Member breathed hard in spite of himself.
Presently the theme was imperceptibly changed. In
the place of despair came hope; in the place of darkness, light. And then she sang, with a voice of such
exquisite sweetness and sympathy, a song of so much
tenderness and simplicity, and so sad, so very sad,
that her listeners were enraptured. Who would
compare a voice on such occasions? It is not that
great singers have lived or do live; it is that there is
always better than the acknowledged best. At least,
so Wingrove thought. There is hope for him if he
will only do the right thing.

He sprang to his feet like one who has suddenly
determined to do something, and who wishes to put
it into execution while yet the spirit is strong upon
him.

" I will see her, Franklin. What do you say ? "

" It would be better."

The Member passed his hand through his beard,
curled his moustache, shook his tie into position, for
these little vanities are with us always, and marched
from the room. Mr. Franklin's eyes followed him
with an ugly look; his brows went close together and
his hands clenched fiercely the arms of the chair. He
shook his head as a dog will when it prepares for
battle, smothered a furious exclamation, mixed himself another whisky and soda, relit his pipe, and sank
back in his arm-chair.

" Ah, Mr. Wingrove," said she, rising from her seat
at the piano as the Member for Billabong entered the
drawing-room, " what a long time it is since we have
seen you ! "

So—she had missed him too.

" Whose fault is that ? " he asked.

" Whose fault should it be but your own ? You
know we are always delighted to see you." She
smiled at him in a manner that fairly took his breath
away. What could this unexpected change mean ?
Had she, then, repented of her folly, or was it some
deceitful female trick ? He knew the sex were always

up to something—it was their way of showing their power. For the moment he doubted the sincerity of her greeting—yet only for the moment. There is that egotism in us which is as fire, and the eyes of women are the fuel thereof. They look into it, and it surges like a forest ablaze; they look away, and it hisses and goes out, as though another deluge had fallen. The strong man trembles, the weak man grows strong, the lame man leaps. There is something in the eyes of a woman, in the curl of her lip, in the curve of her white neck which upsets a man's equanimity. You may be great, or you may only be respectable—a quality too much monopolised by servants—but be you great or little, beautiful or ugly, lean or fat, you will look into a woman's eyes some day, or, more probably, she will look into yours, and you will see something that will set your heart beating, and your blood whirling. Every man has seen this thing, to a greater or a less extent; every man will. It takes many forms, and has many faces, but you will not fail to recognise it, for it is a *real* thing, and when it comes, you will know that there is nothing like it under heaven. And yet in ancient times men treated women with scant courtesy. They were a necessary encumbrance, like the armour worn; softer, truly, but not half so useful. Then came the poets with their golden rhymes, and she became a goddess. What do women not owe these singers ? True, they are surfeited with worship now, but the poet's first great idea remains, and women should never forget that he it was who taught the world her worth. And yet there are some folk who think poets a useless sort of people !

"I have been listening to your singing," said Mr. Wingrove. "It was a treat, Miss Franklin ; a feast for a god."

Mr. Wingrove must surely have seen *that thing* in her eyes, else where did he catch such a fine phrase ?

"I'm afraid you flatter me."

"Do I ?"

"I suppose so. Men used to study flattery once ; foreigners do now, but we English think it insincere. A pity, is it not ?"

She forgot to add that women can flatter too— with the eyes ; a much more dangerous weapon than the sweetest tongue. The eyes will say all that the tongue can tell, and more, much more. Speech is but an impotent, tricky thing after all ; but the eye, in its eloquent way, speaks volumes when the tongue of the most voluble stammers.

"Yes," he said gravely, "it is a pity. One wants sweet language when speaking to, or of, sweet things. Unfortunately, our Parliamentary training teaches us a style the reverse of pleasant. We may be clever, but we must not be flowery."

"But clever people are so insincere."

G

" That's true, because they are never great. All great men are sincere ; all clever men affect sincerity."

She opened her eyes very wide indeed, and watched him with an interest to which she would not have owned. She had determined to meet him and treat him as the best of friends ; draw him out, so to speak, and see how bad he really was. Never a day of the last anxious week had passed without a homily from her father, till she detested the very name of the man whose praises he had sung. But she had never-theless thought deeply ; had gone to bed with a headache, and arisen unrefreshed, till the shadows grew under her eyes and made them luminous, and her heart ached sorely with a great inarticulate pain. Between Stanford and duty yawned a chasm, horrible as the pit of Gehenna, and she was afraid to leap lest she should fall and fearful night close in upon her. Yet here was he who wrung her heartstrings so, speaking with the grace of a courtier, the stateliness of a philosopher ; and she hated him for it.

" Are you always sincere ? " she asked in her quiet way. Women have a way of putting a world of meaning into some of their quiet questions.

" No."

" Are you not afraid of shocking people by such an admission ? "

" Not at all. Nobody is always sincere, and I am only like other people."

"Now you are very insincere in affecting such modesty."

"Indeed, and why ? "

"Papa says you entertain reasonable hopes of the Premiership."

" What man, who is not a clod, has not had his hopes ? If those hopes soar high are they not all the better for that ? "

" But should they fall ? "

" Oblivion will bury them—let it ! At least they have soared, and that is something. Icarus with his folly is better than Diogenes with his tub. I watch the moon by night, the sun by day. Do you know why ? "

" No."

" Because one is beautiful, the other strong, and neither has a rival."

" They are your emblems then ? "

" Precisely."

She grew just a little nervous. There was a deeper meaning in his words than the words conveyed.

" You have my best wishes, Mr. Wingrove. I hope you will succeed."

" If I had you," he said, " I should."

She felt herself grow suddenly hot, then cold ; but she put a good face on and laughed lightly.

" I am but a poor ignorant girl, and not in the least stately and grand like the moon."

G 2

" You have one quality in common."

" And what may that be ? "

" Coldness.   They say the moon is a frozen world ; you must be one of her daughters."

Ah, if he could only have felt the blood that was rushing through that breast, the burning palms, the flushed cheek, he would have told another tale.   Or had he seen her that day with Stanford, when they watched the great sun go down behind Mount Desolation ; had he heard her eager words or watched the fire in her burning eyes, he would not have thought her cold, but would have marvelled at that mystery we call woman.

" Do you know, that is scarcely polite."

" Then you will forgive me, will you not ?   It is a relief to reproach when we are not permitted to praise."

" Oh, I did not mean it," she said, half ashamed of herself.

" I am sure you did not.   But will you sing again ? "

Really !   The request sounded something like presumption.   Yet it was but an ordinary request delivered in a respectful tone.   How different the same words sounded when another spoke them.   She felt angry, she hardly knew why, and would have declined, had she not suddenly remembered that she *must* be agreeable to her visitor.   Had not her father pointed out, a hundred times, that there was everything to be gained by this man's favour—everything to lose by his dislike? She sat down, her fingers flashed over the ivory keys—a bewildering whirl. Mr. Wingrove sat where he could look into her face, his cheek upon his hand, his strange eyes riveted upon her.

"What shall I sing?" she asked.

"That which you sang a few minutes ago."

"Isn't that rather doleful?"

"It was very beautiful."

She struck a soft chord, and played for several moments a tender prelude, then sang the song that had transformed the two hard men into emotional beings. The Member, thoroughly bewildered, sank back intoxicated with the sweet tones.

When he left that night he walked like one in a dream; but before he mounted his horse he said to Mr. Franklin, who had accompanied him out to the gate, "I would give the world to possess her. Believe me, Franklin, you shall never rue the day I lead her to the altar. In a week I will come for my answer. I shall be guided by it. Good-night!" He cut his horse sharply across the shoulder, and was quickly lost in the gloom.

"My dear," said Mr. Franklin as he returned to the drawing-room, "you behaved nobly."

"I did as you told me, papa, though it nearly broke my heart."

"Always do as your father tells you, and you will find him guide you past many a pitfall.   Things will come right in the end, my dear.   I know it's hard upon you, but you will not think so by-and-by. Wingrove is simply infatuated.   He will call this day week for his final answer.   Kiss me, my dear: you are a lucky girl."

"Yes," she said, "I think so."

She held up her burning face, and he pressed his two cold lips to her forehead.

"God bless you, Allie," he said; "you have made me a happy man."

She answered him not, but with a great sob rushed from the room.   He went back to his whisky and soda.

CHAPTER VI.

BENEATH THE STARS.

It was to her bedroom she hurried, but not to sleep, for sleep and she had been enemies of late. Opening her window she leaned her arms on the sill, and looked with tearful eyes out into the still night; up at the moon and stars, away into the Great Beyond. Now was it of her young life she thought; of the mother who had died when she was but a very little thing; of the great world beyond the gloomy mountain, and of the happy fate of other girls and the misery of her own. The tears rushed to her eyes as these various memories came crowding in upon her, and burying her face in her hands she sobbed in a painful, dumb way—an inarticulate grief, stronger by reason of its unspeakableness. She saw the end loom luridly, gloomily, though as yet she dared not speak it to herself. To have admitted the knowledge in spoken words would have been to annihilate hope. Her very muteness seemed to inspire the hope of a reprieve. Then would she try to think of the duty she owed her father; of all that he had done for her, and how even his life depended on her in this crisis. And then of Wingrove would she think, his wealth and his position; of all he could and would do for her and her father. She painted him and his power in the brightest of possible tints, but alas! there was no life in the colours, or life such as made her fearful. "Look," he would say, "you are mine, do you hear? I bought you, I bought you!" And she fancied she could hear the triumphant, masterful ring in his voice, see the glitter in his white-hot eyes; and with a passionate cry of anguish she hid her face in her hands and wept the bitterest tears that ever a young girl shed. Yet what could she do to ward off such a fate? Many things, to be sure, for her love and life were hers. And yet were they? If she fled before the storm she knew that when it broke it would rage with unexampled fury, for ever devastating her own heart. A father ruined, a home destroyed. The picture fixed itself in her brain; it blurred with its ghastly colours her mental vision. It almost drove her mad.

Then a sweet sadness fell upon her as she thought of Stanford. They must part, but she would see him once again and tell him all, and she knew that he would applaud her heroism though it broke his heart. They could still love each other—that she knew they would always do—but they must meet no more. She would honour the name she bore though she died in doing it; and if ever the time came when she could write the words, "I am free!"——. This thought

remained unfinished, even as written here, for it
opened a radiant prospect into which she dared not
peep.

Just then, and while her mind yet trembled lovingly
at the thought, she was startled by the near cry of
a curlew. She arose quickly to her feet, and leaning
out through the window, listened intently. A second,
ten, twenty passed, and then it came again. Her
heart began to beat, her limbs to quiver, and her eyes
shone as though there were more than human fire behind them. A third time came that strange cry. More
prolonged than either of the other two, it seemed to
hang in the air and set it throbbing. A weird cry, an
uncanny thing; more like the wail of a ghost than
anything of the earth. Yet to the anxious listener it
told no such gloomy tale, suggested no such thoughts.
On the contrary, it brought back the warm blood to
her cheeks and, as we have seen, the light to her eyes.
She withdrew with a hasty step to her dressing-table,
seized a box of matches, and struck one, which she
held before the window for a moment. She had
done it often enough before, and someone had
always come and helped her through the window,
and they had walked together beneath the stars; but
now, for the first time, she felt she was doing wrong.
Yet she glided anxiously back to the window with a
beating heart, and presently she heard a soft footfall.
The next moment the creepers at the far end of the

verandah were parted, and a man's figure hastened towards her.

"Tom!"

"Alice!"

The words were only spoken in whispers, but they were of that kind which stir the human heart more than the blare of the trumpet.

"Why have you ventured here?" she asked as soon as he had permitted the freedom of discourse to her lips.

"I wanted to be near you," he said simply.

"But did I not tell you not to come again till I should send for you?"

"Yes," he whispered, "you did; but wild horses could not have kept me back any longer. I had to come, Allie, and I came, so what's the good of talking?"

The girl's heart beat happily, but she said reprovingly, "You have done wrong, Tom."

"Have I, dear? Is doing wrong so sweet as this? If so, I do not wonder that the world is so full of evil-doers. Then all I have hitherto regarded as vice is virtue in disguise, and we are sinners, Allie, you and I?"

"I'm afraid we are, Tom."

"A sweet sinner," he said.

"I won't say this is quite wrong, but I'm sure it isn't quite right."

"Whatever you do is right," he whispered.

She started, like one stung suddenly.

"Will you always think that?" she asked.

"Always, dear."

"Poor Tom!" she thought, "poor Tom!" and dropped her head on his shoulder. But he, unconscious of the thought that regulated this action, stroked her hair and whispered words that were meant for her ear alone.

At length their conversation headed, as it was sure to head, into that channel which they both had striven to avoid: a channel of sunken rocks and horrid quicksands, any one of which might wreck their hopes.

"He has been here again?" said Stanford somewhat suddenly, after a short and painful silence.

"Yes."

"He did not leave till late?"

"You have seen him?"

"Yes."

"And he?"

"Why, you are trembling."

"Did he see you?"

"No. But what kept him here?"

"What should?"

"Allie!"

"I suppose he must have enjoyed the visit."

"Curse him."

" What are curses ? " she asked half coldly. " Do they injure, do they harm, do they bite ? "

" They shall if you wish it."

" Hush ! Don't talk like that. You frighten me."

" Frighten you," he said softly. " Don't you know what you are to me ? Haven't I told you a thousand times ? But, perhaps, I am only a brute of a bushman, and you don't understand me."

" No, no," she answered quickly, " it is not that. I am only afraid that for my sake you may do that of which we shall both repent."

" That's true," he said ; " I would do anything for you. But won't you come out ? " he asked suddenly. " The night is warm, and I have so much to say."

She hesitated for a moment or two, then slipped back into the room and reappeared with a white shawl round her head. Holding out her arms to him he seized her round the waist and lifted her through the window, the sill of which, being but some four feet from the floor of the verandah, rendering the task comparatively easy.

Softly, guiltily, for all the world like a couple of rogues bent on felonious purpose, our lovers stole along the verandah till they reached the corner where the thick screen of creepers fell. Carefully parting this Stanford looked out, and being satisfied with the view, passed through, holding back the leaves for his companion.

"If papa should know," she whispered.

"But he will not." Even if he should, it would not have affected Mr. Stanford much.

She slipped her arm through his, and together they made their way through the long garden—a garden of apples, pears, quinces, grapes, a thousand fruits and flowers—at the bottom of which stood an old summer-house which Alice's mother had built upon her first coming to Koorabyn. Beside, or at the foot of this fragrant edifice, ran the little Warrigal, the stream which rose away out there in the mountains, and which took its name from the fabulous monster of tradition. Little Warrigal did we call it? Well, truly, it was small in summer-time, for then all the country is parched and dry, and the long grass turns to gold, and the rivers and creeks dry up, but you should see it in the winter when the rains are fierce, and the clouds battle and break on the top of Mount Desolation. Then it is a torrent, a foaming, roaring volume of water, seemingly animated, so furious is it, by the fierce spirit of its monstrous deity. Woe betide the unlucky animal that falls into its clutches then. It will make a toothsome dish for the great black dog.

Stanford and Alice stood at the entrance to the arbour, looking silently into the shimmering water at their feet. His arm was thrown around her shoulders, and now and again he would draw her to him—a passionate gesture; but neither spoke for some time, a sadness seeming to have fallen between them. Above, the moon shone in a dark but cloudless sky; millions upon millions of stars glistened; great patches of stars, a thousand milky ways — as though the Almighty had flung them over the face of the firmament by handfuls. Among the reeds the frogs croaked their sad hymns to the night, and the soft breezes stirred the leaves, making a low, sweet sound.

"How strange and lonely it is," she said. "If the Black Warrigal were only a reality, I should expect to see him rise from the water on such a night as this."

He laughed, but even that sounded odd. It was not a night for laughter. There is something indescribably solemn about these Australian nights. If you give your fancy rein you will soon approach the supernatural, for in those vast solitudes you unconsciously draw nearer to God—are impelled onward, as it were. There are no sphinxes here, no pyramids to connect the living with the dead; you are with the unknown always. It is vast, incomprehensible, but it stirs the imagination, and teaches man to think. Yet this same moon shone in the valley of Ajalon as it does to-night, shone on the just and unjust, and

listened to many a tale of love, of hate and terror.
How coldly it smiles at the recollection, if it recollect
at all; for long ere Ajalon was named had it not seen
and heard the like? Of all those lips flushed with
burning words, of all those loves, of all those hates—
what is there left? Into the form of clay is breathed
the divine fire; it glows for a moment like a god, and
is consumed with its own glory. And what then?
Tell us, O moon! The sun that stood still on Gibeon
and lighted Joshua to revenge is the same sun that
we saw go down behind Mount Desolation. Since
time itself has it looked down upon those mighty solitudes, perhaps not always solitudes. Needs it then so
great a stretch of imagination to picture this grim
land in the old dead ages, when men have been and
are, and always shall be the same? The lips that
kissed, the hands that caressed, the hearts that
warred! Why, if it so please you, you shall see,
whenever the moon floods the great weird forests
with its spectral light, the ghosts of the long-departed
dancing fantastically in the shadows of the ghostly
trees.

Stanford led the girl to a seat within the summer-
house and began to question her of the things so near
his heart, for what to him was the sun of Joshua, or the
moon that held her lamp above the valley of Ajalon?
Filled with an all-consuming thought, he plied her
with a thousand questions.

"He came," she said in answer to one of his numerous queries, "and had a long talk with papa, in which, I believe, they discussed my future and disposed of me in a competent and thoroughly business-like way." She laughed somewhat bitterly as she spoke. Stanford groaned. "Then," she continued, almost flippantly her companion thought, "he was good enough to come into the drawing-room and request me to entertain him. And really, Tom, he astonished me with his ready talk and good manners —a little abrupt at times, but quite good enough for all that."

Truly there must be something feline in woman's nature—that is when the cat is in a cheerful mood, before it gobbles up the little mouse with which it has amused itself. Stanford ground his teeth with jealous fury.

"If I had him here," he said, "I'd twist his neck, the impudent rascal! But tell me all, dear, tell me all."

"What can I tell that you do not know or guess? I made myself agreeable for papa's sake, and I'm afraid he fell deeper in love than ever." It is always a satisfaction to let your lover know that he is not the only one who regards you as a divinity. It quickens his perception and shows him what a lucky fellow he really is. Though why Alice should have aggravated poor Tom's wretchedness, knowing how

well he loved her, exceeded mortal comprehension—
unless the bitterness of her own heart took a gruesome
delight in inflicting pain on someone, no matter
whom.

"Well," he replied, meekly enough in all conscience, "I do not wonder at that, dear, for who
could help loving you? But it is terrible to think
that you should be subject to such humiliations while
I, who would lay down my life for you, must stir no
hand or foot. Have you thought over what I proposed? Will you let me go to your father? Surely,
if I tell him all, he will see that a union such as he
proposes is as unjust as it is infamous?"

"It is too late. My father is as powerless to move
as I. We are in his grip and must abide our fate. I
have struggled, have schemed as no girl ever schemed
before, but my struggles have been in vain, and my
schemings have but shown me my own impotence.
Things have gone too far, Tom. It might have been
once, but now it is too late. This day week he will
return to me for his final answer."

There was a coldness, a tone of cynicism in her
voice which he did not like.

"What do you mean by that?" he asked.

"I mean that he will return for a 'yes' or 'no'—
either of which shall be irrevocable."

"There can be no question, no doubt as to which
it will be?"

H

She felt the strong arm about her tremble, the hand that clasped her own quiver.

"Tom," she replied, looking up into his face, "you know what we are to each other, how much I love you; you know that I would give anything to place my hand in yours and go out into the world with you. It has been the dream of my life since—since the first time you told me all that was in your heart and made me, oh, so happy."

"My dear one!"

"But love is a selfish thing, Tom, and sees no further than the beloved one's eyes. I forgot, we forgot, that there are others for whom we must work, for whom we must live. It seemed to me as though there were nothing in life but to sit and dream, and I dreamt like one in paradise. But I am awake now; the dream is flown. I have learnt my duty."

"Do you mean, Allie," he said, in a low, passionate voice, "that you will give yourself to this man? Give yourself to him—think of it! Ruin your life— my life!—blast our hopes here and hereafter for this fantastic whim of yours! Your duty is to the man you love; your father has no right to claim this sacrifice. It is scandalous—infamous! Were he a man of one courageous thought, one atom of spirit, he would starve, die, ere he would sanction such an outrage."

"You do not know papa."

He laughed harshly. "And yet he would sell you as he would a bale of wool."

"Well, what then?"

"What then!" he echoed; "with you it is everything."

"Are there not other bales of wool?"

"Pardon me!"

"I have nothing to pardon. So that the bale brings good value, what more is wanting?"

"But you—you?"

"It may break my heart, but it will save our home and my father from dishonour."

"Then when he comes——?"

"My answer will be 'yes.'"

He drew her suddenly to him as though he were afraid they might drag her from him then.

"You cannot," he cried, "by heaven you cannot!"

Through a break in the trees overhead the bright moon shone down on them, the stars smiled in their inscrutable way. What was it, after all, this tale of love? Had they not seen the like since the first man looked upon the beauty of woman? From east to west, from north to south, from the wickedness of Gomorrah to the holy calm of the Egyptian Laura, it was ever the same—for who shall strive with nature? What recked those watchers of a sigh, of a broken heart? They had heard the same tale whispered in the gardens of Babylon, and ages before

Babylon lifted its proud towers to the sky. A pressure of the hand, a look into the eyes, a kiss, and for life and death these two were one. An inexplicable race these mortals! No wonder the stars twinkled merrily as they watched, though their queen sailed on in her beautiful, passionless way.

"But, Allie," continued the young man earnestly, "you cannot love—you have no affection for this man ?"

"No," she cried with an hysterical laugh, "I am selling myself."

Stanford shuddered.

"It cannot be, it must not! By heaven, it shall not!"

"You see, Tom," she said, with the same little, excited laugh, a laugh that troubled him even more than her words, for it was reckless to a degree, "you see, my market value is three thousand pounds, that is the least that can be taken, though I may fetch twenty thousand more—not bad for a bale of wool, is it? Yet for a poor man three thousand is a fortune as unobtainable as Aladdin's lamp. I am afraid you are too poor to purchase such a jewel."

"Don't taunt me with my poverty. I never knew the curse of it till now. Three thousand pounds, you say; that is the sum advanced ?"

"Yes. Do you think me worth so much ?" She

laughed more cynically than ever. She was excited, hysterical.

" You are all the world to me."

" Poor old Tom."

" Three thousand pounds," he repeated ; " three thousand pounds ! It would free you, dear ? "

" As it now binds me."

" And I have not three hundred to my name."

" You could not get it ? "

" No. I have no property, and in these days they will not take a bond on one's soul."

" Then we need fight no more." Her tone of hopeless resignation maddened him.

" Is there no way, no way ? "

" None. It is our fate and we must bow to it. We have been living in dreams, Tom, and dwelling in a palace of air. The dream is now a grim reality, and our palace has melted in the sunlight. We must part now, Tom ; it is not to be."

" Ah," he cried, " you do not love me ; you would never be so cruel."

She flung her arms round his neck and kissed him passionately. All her soul went out to him at that moment, and he knew it.

" There," she said, panting as she spoke, " that is how I love you. You are all the world to me, and in parting from you I abandon every hope of happiness. There, there, say nothing, but go. Perhaps you will soon forget me. There are many prettier girls than I, and you may love one all the better for having known me."

" There is none but you," he said.

" As for me," she continued, though her voice quivered as with intense strain, " I know not how I shall bear it, or what the world will think of me, or how my own heart will shudder at myself, but I shall know—may the thought give me consolation—that I have done my duty."

"Sad duty," he muttered.

" When a soldier dies at his post you call him a brave man ; can't you spare a little praise for me ? But perhaps you think I may not be called upon for the sacrifice ?"

" Who knows ?" he said.

She marked the tone and pitied him the sudden hope.

" Poor boy !" she said. " It is a dream. Good-bye !"

He placed a hand on each of her shoulders and looked eagerly into her face.

" Why should we part ?"

" You forget," she said.

" I forget nothing."

" Tom, Tom !" There was so much pain in her voice that he quivered like one beneath the lash. Flinging himself at her feet he clasped her round the waist.

" Forgive me, oh, forgive me ! "

" Yes, yes." She drew his head to her and smoothed his hair with gentle hands. "And I will forget too. Come, dear, do not give way to grief like this. Let us hope to the last."

He arose, and taking the hand she offered, pressed it passionately to his lips. Then folding it between his own he said, "You would marry me, dear, but for this awful debt."

" Yes, yes."

" And your father ? "

" Would be happy too, for I know he secretly detests Mr. Wingrove, but he cannot move hand or foot. Oh, Tom, Tom, why did we ever meet ? "

" Don't speak like that," he said, " because our love has been to me most precious. The crown of the world were nothing by its side. If we never meet again you will remember that, won't you ? You will remember that I loved you so well that there was nothing I would not do to make you happy. You will remember that I shall go through the world with your name on my lips, and that my last thought shall be of you." The girl sobbed loudly as he spoke. "Come, come," he continued, "you have been courageous so far, you must not break down now. I would have led you from your noble resolve a moment ago. It was another of my many errors. Forget it. Courage and hope. Perhaps Heaven will not permit the sacrifice.   And now one last request.   You must not give your promise till the appointed day."

"I promise," she sobbed ; " I promise."

"This day week ? "

" Yes, yes."

"Till then courage and hope.   God bless you, dear —good-night !"

A passionate kiss, a heart-bursting sob, a woman's flying form, a man standing irresolute, and a cold, white moon above.

CHAPTER VII.

HOW THE WOOROOTA BANK WAS "STUCK UP."

WOOROOTA was one of the most flourishing towns of
the north-eastern district, and in the opinion of its
inhabitants was even more flourishing than statistics
proved. This exaltation of one's belongings, so to
speak, is, however, an amiable prejudice and easily
pardoned. When the inhabitant, therefore, of this
particular town declared that it was a "grand place,"
there was no doubt whatever of his sincerity, and a
sincere man should always be listened to with respect.
Frenchmen honestly believe that Paris is the centre
of the world, though to millions it is but a vague
name; to thousands its very existence is unknown.
The Englishman honestly believes that he is better
than his erring brother; and the American just as
honestly imagines that he can "lick creation." These,
as we have said, are all amiable little weaknesses;
they please the patriot and they do no harm. Therefore let them flourish, since they flatter the national
vanity, for vanity in a nation—or pride, which is the
most dignified form of vanity—as in men and women,
is conducive to much good. Pride is a much more
agreeable sensation than shame, and if the Wooroo-

taite was proud of his growing city it would be a thankless, and perhaps dangerous, task to attempt to dissuade him from such an absurd idea.

We are then, out of deference to its inhabitants, prepared to admit that Wooroota was a "grand place." Its main street was such as few cities could boast, being broad enough to accommodate an army; its side streets were almost as wide, thereby offering great facilities to the dust fiend for his merry revels. The Woorootaites avoided crowding as they would the plague; land was cheap and they used it prodigally. It was quite a journey to cross that main street of theirs, and if you were not lost in a dust-storm in the middle of it, you risked being run over by a galloping horse, for it was not an infrequent thing to see the merry bushmen careering up and down the thoroughfare utterly oblivious of the fact that they were not upon the broad plains of the Riverina. These antics, however, interfered not with the vehicular traffic of the town, for beyond an occasional bullock waggon, which naturally engaged a considerable space, and, if the driver was in a merry mood, attention also, there was not much regulating of traffic required.

Wooroota lay on the main road to Sydney, and in the early days, long before the prodigious thought of an intercolonial railway had permeated the public mind, it enjoyed no little renown in its own little way for not alone was it a great pastoral centre, but it was the headquarters of the police as well, and when there was any bushranging going on, it presented a striking and animated appearance. Then the place literally swarmed with troopers, and trade flourished in consequence; for troopers have to be fed, and as the Government feeds them it has to pay doubly for the privilege. But, alas! there were no bushrangers at large in the piping times of which we write. The last gang had but lately been exterminated amid scenes of absorbing horror, and their fate had taught such a lesson to all would-be malefactors that there seemed to be none left with spirit enough to bail up a gum tree. The troopers were once more dispersed about the country, and Wooroota had to rest content with its cattle shows, its market days, and its race week. It is true the place grew somewhat merry of a Saturday night, but it was not of that kind which delighteth the gentle soul; for at the hospital they generally had two or three new patients every Sunday morning. Of course, there was the railway station for those who were fond of a little mild excitement. The trains between Melbourne and Sydney stopped here for a quarter of an hour while the travellers alighted to refresh the inner man, or woman, as the sex might be, and as the hurrying, bustling passengers crowded to and from the refreshment rooms, they usually afforded the onlooking Woorootas a fund of innocent pleasure. Was there not sure to be some old lady who could not find her carriage; some old gentleman who argued the time with the guard; some gentleman of any age who left things till the last moment and only succeeded in getting on board the train by the skin of his teeth? Then you should see the Woorootas grin—it is so amusing to see a man make a fool of himself. We laugh till we are stiff at the antics of the novice on horseback, but we may be sure that it is a solemn enough business to him.

Of the buildings, public or private, we need not here dilate, as it will be taken for granted that everything in the architectural line was stately and beautiful; and if the Roman Catholic Cathedral was built of zinc, the Wesleyan chapel of wood, the Bunyip Hotel there at the corner was of massive granite, and gave quite a solid and respectable appearance to the neighbourhood. Then there was the post-office, a grand, glaring, and very lovely red-brick edifice of which the town was particularly proud, and of which the sun seemed particularly fond, for it clung to it like a young lover to the lips of his mistress. It is true that next to this magnificent building there was a tumble-down blacksmith's shop, before which profane bushmen lounged and smoked and swore while their horses were being shod; but this, instead of detracting from that stately pile, gave to it an increase of dignity, and from the first-floor windows

the postmaster's wife and daughter surveyed the surrounding city with something like a pitying smile.

There was, however, one rival to the post-office,
and that was the Union Bank. In England they
think first of the money: in Australia it is different.
There they first think of the building. Any bank
that is a bank would suffer terribly unless it could
transact its business in one of the noblest edifices of
the town. The Bank of England might pass muster
because its name is associated with unbounded wealth,
and it has a gorgeous beadle in its courtyard whom
the bushman might mistake for the Lord Mayor:
but he would not trust a five-pound note of his in
such a mean-looking edifice as Coutts's—they might
stick to it !

The Union Bank, then—a solid brick building
plastered over so as to resemble stone—as we have
said, rivalled the post-office, and, so its owner thought,
beat it too, though that, as the postmaster's wife
could tell you, was a matter of opinion. It, however,
had a better and more central position than the last-
named building, for it was exactly opposite the
Bunyip Hotel, and therefore fair in the centre of
the town. It was, moreover, a corner building, and
had an ornamental verandah round it which afforded
shelter to the weary and the lazy. At the junction of
the two main streets, it was, of course, in the busiest
portion of the town, so that the tramp of feet, the

clatter of vehicles, was a sound which occasionally, if not incessantly, fell upon the ears of its inmates. But the town was busier this week than usual on account of the show. Farmers great and small jostled each other and nodded good-day; bushmen galloped up and down the great street, raising clouds of dust, and many a good man lay stretched beneath the shade of a verandah in a shocking state of intoxication. The place, in fact, was full of a nondescript class, of horses and carts, buggies and waggonettes, so that when two tall, bearded men drove up to the bank in a light two-wheeled gig, or dog-cart, alighted and made the pony fast to a ring in one of the verandah poles, no one who saw them thought their actions worthy of a head turn, so passed on.

It had indeed been a busy week in Wooroota, and Mr. Parsons, as he leant back on his stool, pensively chewing the end of his pen and staring vacantly at the open book before him, in which were arrayed a series of bewildering figures, cursed the show in a dreamy sort of way—it gave him so much work—and wondered if that big fly on the window could possibly buzz much longer. Mr. Parsons had just shut up shop—we beg his pardon, had just closed the bank—and had returned to his desk to cast up his figures, a proceeding which was necessary before he left the office for the day. But, as we have seen, there was not much energy in his eyes, for he was thinking sadly of his wasted life, and was wondering if he was really doomed to an ignoble stool in a far-away country town. The fly in the window buzzed loudly as if to say "yes" to his wonderings, which so angered him that he began in a languid way to chew the blotting paper into little pellets which he flung feebly at the irritating insect. This effort seemed somewhat to relieve his pent-up feelings, and he worked assiduously for about two minutes; then he stopped again and began to chew his pen in the same dreamy manner. He wondered how he survived so much hard work. He was not a strong man, physically, having a wrist as genteel as a bank clerk's should be, and a long thin hand, the delicate fingers of which had never wielded a more formidable weapon than a billiard cue. Yet they worked him as though he were a bullock, as he told Mr. Brown, his manager, often. But Brown, who was of a sporting turn, and went to Melbourne regularly for the Cup, merely laughed at him in a brutal sort of way and said it would do him good. But then Brown had a constitution like a prize-fighter and was never so happy as when he was busy; though if you were to ask Mr. Parsons he would tell you that the manager's happiest and busiest times were usually spent *outside* the bank.

Mr. Parsons was, however, working hard as we have seen, as was the fly in the window, for he made so great a buzzing that the clerk looked up quite furious—

for him. Really, he could not tolerate the nuisance any longer. He would despatch that fly if he perished in the attempt. Seizing his ruler he slipped from his perch and advanced stealthily towards the enemy, who, unconscious of approaching danger, hummed with a loud delight. Mr. Parsons' eyes sparkled with anticipated victory as he stepped silently onward; but when just opposite the door he gave a sudden jump, for someone outside had knocked thereon.

"Confound these bumpkins," cried Mr. Parsons angrily, "they think a man is at their disposal all hours of the day and night. What do you want?" he asked sharply as he opened the door.

There were two tall, bearded men standing on the steps, and as the door opened one of them advanced with an open cheque in his hand.

"Would you be good enough to cash this cheque?" As he spoke, the man imperceptibly encroached upon the open doorway. His companion moved with him.

"Can't," said Mr. Parsons sharply. "You ought to know what time the bank closes." He prepared to shut the door, as much as to say "that will do for you," but, somehow, the applicant's knee had got against it.

"You would oblige me very much," continued the man in a humble tone.

"Can't be done," said the clerk. "Bank's closed."

"But I am leaving Wooroota this afternoon," the man went on, ignoring Mr. Parsons' refusal, "and it will put me to considerable inconvenience and expense if I have to stay on."

"That's none of my business."

"Are you the manager, sir?"

"No—a—that is a—I'm his assistant, you see."

"Where is he then? Let me see him. I am sure he will not refuse so slight a favour."

"Well, if you want to see him you had better call to-morrow, for he went to Jorong to-day." Jorong was a cheerful little place about seventeen miles away.

The man and his companion had, during this conversation, worked forward inch by inch till he who held the cheque in his hand had got one shoulder half way through the partly opened door. A smile lit up his dark face as the clerk vouchsafed this piece of information, and pushing forward suddenly he and his companion slipped swiftly into the bank. The companion closed the door and locked it with a chuckle. Ere Mr. Parsons could recover from his astonishment at this piece of audacity, he found himself looking into the muzzle of a revolver.

"Bail up!" cried the man sternly. "Throw your hands up!"

This "bail up" of the Australian bushranger was usually followed by the second command, "Throw your hands up," and woe betide the rash being who

I

disobeyed it, or sought for some weapon with which to defend himself. Ere he could move, a bullet would crash through his brain. But if the command was instantly obeyed no harm would befall the victim, for the bushranger's object was invariably plunder, and so that he met no opposition, he rarely, or never, stained his hands with blood. Even he, in his lawless state, seemed to have a horror of murder, as have all civilised men. But let him meet armed opposition and he would fight like a fury, and if his natural enemies, the police, came in contact with him, hate of the direst nature directed the bullets from both sides. There was no worm so loathsome as a trooper, no vermin so fit to be crushed; on the other hand, the trooper knew it was a battle to the death between them, and that victory meant no little glory and a substantial reward. The outlaw fought only to escape the rope.

As soon as Mr. Parsons saw that horrid weapon pointed at his head, and heard those dreadful words, an intense nervousness seized him and he felt like falling to the floor. The ruler, with which he had meant to exterminate that obnoxious fly, flew from his trembling grasp and rolled away to one corner, and though he strove to obey the order he could not from sheer fright.

"Come," said the man fiercely, "up with your hands!"

Mr. Parsons thought he heard the click of the revolver; he could already feel the bullet crashing through his brain. Up, like lightning, went his two hands above his head.

"That's right," smiled the man with the pistol; "keep them there and you're safe enough. We don't want to hurt you, mate, our business is of another kind; but if you utter a sound, or give any sort of alarm, you are a dead man." The clerk groaned aloud, but held his arms up to their extreme height— a difficult task for one of his physique, but, under existing circumstances, one which he performed right nobly.

"Search him," said the man to his companion.

This was done under cover of the revolver, though had there been no such weapon the task would have been as easy. Mr. Parsons could not have tackled the fly at that moment.

There was nothing of consequence in the clerk's pockets but a bunch of keys, which were immediately handed over to him who had done all the talking and who appeared to be the chief.

"Now," said that gentleman, addressing the clerk, "you may put your hands down. It must be pretty hard work for a fellow like you to keep them up. I'm sorry to have thus inconvenienced you, but necessity—you can guess the rest. First of all tell me, is there anyone upstairs?"

I 2

"Yes," answered the clerk in a quivering voice, "the—the missis and two children."

"No servant?"

"She—she's laid up with the me—measles."

"That's all right. Now listen to me Mr.—what's your name?"

"Pa—arsons."

"Then listen to me, Mr. Parsons. We want to transact our little bit of business as quietly as possible. I have no wish to disturb the missis nor the children, do you understand? Besides, I have left my card-case at home on the piano, so cannot think of calling. Now show us where you keep the money, and mind, no tricks. If you attempt any you are a dead man. If however, you behave yourself, you are as safe as though you were out yonder in the police barracks. We are desperate, you understand, and will have no trifling. Now then, here are the keys—where is the money?"

Mr. Parsons took the keys in his trembling fingers, making them jingle as he did so, and led the two men into an inner room, where stood a gigantic safe. This was quickly opened, and its gold and notes smartly transferred into two bags which the robbers had brought with them.

"How much is there?" asked the chief, his grey eyes glittering with a strange light as he surveyed the enormous wealth.

"I can't say to a few hundreds," was the reply of the clerk, whose confidence was returning with the knowledge that he was safe ; "I was just balancing my books when you entered."

"Well, well, how much ?" asked the man impatiently.

"A good lot," said the clerk. "You see, the squatters and cockatoos have deposited largely on account of the show."

"How much ?" cried the man angrily.

Mr. Parsons thought he heard that deadly click again.

"Between three and four thousand," he answered hastily. "Nearer four than three."

"Ah !" The great sigh escaped the man ere he knew it. With an angry and impatient gesture, as though to hide the effect the knowledge of this sum had produced upon him, he turned to the clerk— "You have done very well so far, Mr. Parsons ; but there are the books—we must not leave them !"

"They are of little use," suggested the clerk.

"No matter."

In a moment they were all ablaze.

"Now," said the chief, "we have only one more task for you. Do as you have done and we shall get on very well together. We have a trap outside, and want you to come for a drive with us. We've seen so little of each other, Mr. Parsons, that I am loth to part with you. Will you come with us, or shall we bind and gag you?"

"I will go with you."

"A very sensible determination. Besides, I shouldn't like to hurt you, and to gag you would seem unfriendly. You might die before morning. Now understand what you are to do." He dropped his flippant tone and spoke seriously, his companion looking on with an amused, half-wondering grin. "You will carry that big bag; my mate 'll look after the little one; I'll look after you. You must lock up everything as usual, and go out and take your seat beside us; if anyone should come up, you are going for a drive with a couple of your friends."

"I understand."

"We shall have to drive through the town. A hundred opportunities of betraying us will present themselves to you; but remember that I shall have a hand on my revolver, and if by look or nod you cause us to be suspected, I swear to you that I will put a bullet through your brain. We are desperate men, you understand, and must not be thwarted. On the other hand, if you give us no cause for suspicion, you have nothing to fear. Now let us go."

Mr. Parsons took up the big bag, the chief's companion the smaller one, and they prepared to issue from the building, the chief first of all looking through the window to see that the trap was safe and the coast clear. Unfortunately, for them, that part of the bank in which their operations had taken place looked on one street only, but finding that clear they trusted the rest to Providence.

Mr. Parsons led them to the private entrance and opened the street door. The chief's companion was the first to emerge. With a complacent air he stepped forth, the bag under his arm, and in another moment it was safe beneath the seat of the trap. He then mounted into the driver's place, took the whip and reins in his hands, and sat as calmly there as though he were in church. The clerk was the next to appear, the big bag in his possession. He looked very pale and excited, but as he was cadaverous-looking by nature, it is probable that no one would have noticed the extra paleness. The chief emerged almost at the same time, closing the door softly behind him. Not a sound, all this time, had come from the people up-stairs, at which the robbers marvelled much, but which was explained afterwards by the fact that the manager's wife and children were fast asleep at the time. In a moment the bag was transferred from the clerk's hands into those of the man who held the reins; the next moment it disappeared beneath the seat. Almost simultaneously two troopers strolled round the corner of the street which the robber chief had been unable to reconnoitre. The man with the reins gave an almost inaudible grunt; the clerk breathed a sigh of relief, but lifting up his eyes he encountered a dreadful look in the bushranger's face.

"Remember!" he hissed.

"Off for a drive, Mr. Parsons?" asked one of the troopers, advancing to the edge of the kerb.

"Yes," replied the clerk with a ghastly sort of smile. "A couple of my friends just come round to give me a lift. It isn't every day I get such a chance as this."

"Ah, well," replied the trooper, "you'll be a manager soon." And smiling knowingly at his companion the two guardians of the peace moved on.

"That was very well played, Mr. Parsons," said the bushranger, motioning the clerk to mount and then mounting beside him. "He didn't understand the joke, though, did he?" The clerk smiled sadly by way of reply, the driver chuckled—indeed, he did nothing but chuckle—whipped up his horse, and away they went.

They drove through the most busy part of the town unmolested, past the police barracks, where they saw several troopers, then out into the open country. Now they all breathed freely for the first time, and Mr. Parsons saw that right hand removed from that awful breast pocket. He felt infinitely relieved at that little action, and when he saw the bushrangers take out their pipes and begin to smoke he knew that they intended him no harm. His spirits rose wonderfully, he felt a hero, he hardly knew why. Perhaps he knew that in twenty-four hours his name would be in every mouth in Australia. Certainly a very gratifying reflection.

"I say," he said at last, feeling exceedingly cheerful and curious, and contemplating all he would have to tell the world by-and-by, "you did it pretty neatly, didn't you?"

"We always do," replied the man. The driver chuckled in his inscrutable way.

"You are not a couple of the Kellys, are you?" asked the clerk. Certainly, he must get as much information as possible. He would be in great demand presently: his name on everyone's lips. The office stool had brought him glory at last.

"We are their ghosts," replied the chief.

"No, but," continued Mr. Parsons earnestly, "I have a theory about the Kellys, a theory of my own, don't you know, which you may help me to prove."

"I shall be very pleased to oblige one who has been so obliging."

"Then I should like to know if you really did belong to them?"

"Were they not annihilated?" asked the chief mysteriously.

"They were *supposed* to be," was the reply; "and, indeed, Ned was hanged in Melbourne, if you recollect; but what about Dan and the other two?"

He asked this with a triumphant smile. He forgot
that he was arguing with a bushranger—one who might
suddenly take it into his head to put a bullet through
him—and that to talk of hanging in such company
was not an agreeable, though perhaps appropriate,
topic.

"Were their bones not found after the shanty was
burnt down?" asked the man in the same mysterious
tone. "Didn't they perish like rats in a trap?"

"They found *some* bones," said the clerk significantly.

"Well," said the man with a grim laugh, "we are
those bones."

The driver gave a loud guffaw; a chuckle, however great, could not have expressed his feelings.

"You may or may not be those bones," said the
clerk with as much dignity as he dared assume—
though you should hear him snap his customers when
they call—"but it doesn't interfere with my theory
all the same."

"What is your theory?" asked the chief with an
amused smile.

"It's this," replied Mr. Parsons seriously. "No
one knows that the bones found after the fire were
the bones of the Kellys. If one of their number
could escape from the house, why couldn't they all?"

"Why, indeed?" repeated the man. "There was
no reason why they shouldn't, and you may bet your

life they did. The bones they found were those of three poor swagmen."

"I knew it," cried the clerk triumphantly. "I knew it. Then you are they—the Kellys?"

"We are."

He who was driving leant suddenly forward and administered a sharp cut to the horse, but even that effort could not stifle his merriment. Leaning back in his seat he laughed aloud, his companion smiling in a serious sort of way; but the clerk looked on with an unmoved countenance. He was satisfied, and never stooped to ask himself a single question. The mind that knows its own greatness never doubts, never changes. Like a rock it defies both waves and wind. It will bow to nothing but its own opinions.

After this hilarious outburst the trio drove on for some time in silence in the same north-westerly direction, till at last they drew up at the junction of two roads.

"We must say good-bye here," said the chief of the bushrangers, addressing the clerk; "jump down."

Mr. Parsons did as he was bidden. They were about ten miles from Wooroota at that point.

"I'm afraid you'll have to walk back," continued the man, "but it won't hurt you after being cramped up in your office all day. And now I have one further request to make. You must accept no offer of a lift, however many you may get; for, you understand, we anticipate a good chase, and therefore require a good start. I shall know whether you have obeyed me or not. Look to it if you don't."

The clerk declared that he would obey the command to the letter.

"You see," went on the bushranger, "I might tie you up, gag you, put a bullet through you. But you have done me no harm, and I don't want to do you any. As soon as you reach the barracks you may inform the police. Don't forget to give them my kindest regards,.and above all things, tell them that I consider they have been extremely negligent." With that he waved his hand ; his companion shook the reins, and away they went, leaving the clerk standing in the middle of the road. For a while he watched them as they bowled along in a cloud of dust, then a turn in the road hid them from his sight. With a sigh he began his homeward journey.

The robbers, in the meantime, had driven the trap into the bush, where they stopped and alighted ; and while he who appeared to be the chief went hastily through the plunder, the driver disappeared into a bit of thick scrub, and a few minutes after reappeared leading two splendid-looking saddle horses. Little was said by the men, but the leader, who had apparently divided the money very unequally, handed the smaller portion to his companion, and made his own share fast to his saddle. Then they seized each other by the hand without speaking, though a look passed between them deeper than words. The next moment they were in their saddles and away. Each took a southerly course, though one went so as to pass to the east of Wooroota, the other to the west.

They had driven from the town in a northerly direction.

[NOTE.—*This robbery is founded on an incident in the career of the Kelly Gang.*]

CHAPTER VIII.

AN INTERRUPTION.

THE sixth day was duly ushered in, the end of the period of grace. As Alice looked from her window that morning at the newly-arisen sun she upbraided it for giving promise of such a glorious day. It had no right to shine as if in bitter mockery of her woes. To-day she was to speak that word which was to change the whole tenor of her life, perhaps wreck it —it could do little else. Furious and, at times, almost evil thoughts rushed through her brain. How could she respect or honour a man of so little principle—a man who was willing to take her and make her his wife knowing well that she neither honoured nor respected him, and that her heart was given to another? And in the contemplation of her hatred for him she seemed to forget that honour and respect which she owed herself. Though only for a moment. She would be true to her vows, yes! She would never look on Stanford's face again. The past should be blotted from her memory. Let them come. She was ready.

All that day she wandered about the house like one but half awake, trembling at the sound of every footstep, the ring of every voice. The fall of a horse's hoof, the barking of a dog, the shutting of a door— any of these continual occurrences caused her nerves to flutter and the blood to stand still about her heart. She tried to read, to sleep, but could not. She put on her hat and went down to the summer-house, where she and Stanford had parted a week ago. She sat where they had sat, and pictured the sad, happy scene over and over again. The picture maddened her, and she arose with a little scream. At her feet lay the placid waters of the Warrigal. A wild sickening thought rushed through her; but with a wave of her hand, as though to push it from her, she hurried from the place. She could not breathe in it; the atmosphere seemed too heavily laden with the memories which she must forget.

The afternoon passed, and still he came not for his answer. Why, she wondered. For a moment a wicked, joyful thought was hers. Had anything befallen him? Yet she hid it away from her as best she could. She did not mean that, no, no! After all, was not his only crime his love for her? Perhaps his better nature had revolted against this perpetration of wrong, had pointed out the sin he would commit, and he had gone away, and they would hear from him soon telling of his sudden decision. Yet she gained little comfort from this thought; she could not make it seem real. Her hopes pulled one way with her heart, her knowledge the other. No, he would come, he would come!

And come he did, for the heavens never fall for the benefit of the condemned. The sun was just sinking behind Mount Desolation when the sound of hoofs was heard, and Mr. Wingrove was seen advancing. Mr. Franklin went out to meet him as usual, and shook him warmly by the hand, talking glibly as he led him back into the drawing-room.

"I must congratulate you, Wingrove," he said as he encountered the interrogating eye of the Member. "She has learnt to appreciate the magnanimity of your offer, and a—well, I must leave the rest to you."

Mr. Wingrove smiled rather curiously. "Did she say so?"

"Perhaps not quite in those words. You know girls have a quiet way of expressing themselves, but they mean a lot, don't you know." Mr. Franklin laughed; not so his companion, who appeared to be very serious and not a little agitated.

"You know, Franklin, if I thought she wasn't satisfied," he began.

"Satisfied, my dear fellow, my daughter is a sensible girl."

"I had believed so."

Mr. Wingrove sat down and surveyed his companion with his steady, scrutinising gaze, and that gentleman rather shifted under it, for he read in it something not complimentary to himself. He had, however, made several visits to his study that day, so that his courage was in excellent condition, and he chatted on as though the event was of no consequence whatever. Then he arose with a mysterious smile, begged to be excused, and departed. Wingrove arose also with a gesture of impatience and began to pace the room.

Mr. Franklin, in the meantime, walked direct to his daughter's apartment, knocked gently upon the door and entered. He found her sitting in a listless attitude by the window, a book in her lap, her hands toying thoughtlessly with its leaves.

" He has come, dear," her father whispered.

She looked up into his eyes but said nothing. Yet as he saw that look of anguish his heart smote him sorely, selfish as he was.

" Allie," he said, stooping and kissing her, noticing, too, the little shudder that swept through her frame, " you are a brave girl, you have saved our honour. For months I have been dwelling in a more than Egyptian gloom, afraid to breathe, to move a single step. But now I see the sun again, I grasp peace and happiness. God bless you, child; you have saved your father's life."

She smiled bitterly.

" At what price ? " she asked coldly, looking out through the window as she spoke.

" Price," he echoed, " I do not understand you."

J

"I should have thought you did. Shall I speak more plainly?" she asked almost sternly, and looked as though she would.

"My child," he answered soothingly, "I don't deny your right to anger, for you have been crossed in your plans by necessity, and you naturally hate it in consequence. Yet believe me, my dear, that when your indignation has abated, and you have calmly considered the many excellent points of this action, you will wonder why you ever hesitated."

"Perhaps so. At any rate it will make no difference then. Yet I must tell you, father, that I shall not live to wear his ring, and that I hate him with all my soul."

"Tut, tut, child, this is sheer romantic folly. No girl can hate a man with so much money. Possibly, he may not be the husband I would have chosen for you, but I assure you that you exaggerate his—deficiencies." He brought out this last word with an effort. How a man with such wealth could be deficient in any quality exceeded his comprehension. We are afraid that Mr. Franklin was just a little sordid.

"You are as full of romance," he went on, "as any fool of a poet. Where you found it in a confounded country like this is a thing that puzzles me. I can't see it for the life of me. Fancy a girl like you thinking she loved that lout Stanford! It's ridiculous in the first place, and undignified in the second."

"I think we had better leave dignity out of the question. As for my folly, as you call it, we must leave that to God. I only know that I love Stanford with all my soul."

"Well, well," he replied, "if that is so I am sorry, though I still believe that you, unconsciously, exaggerate your affection. Stanford was a very good servant, but hardly a husband for my daughter. Why, it was as much as he could do to keep himself."

The girl smiled disdainfully. "But could he have paid the mortgage on Koorabyn?"

"My dear," was the reply, "you are asking a perfectly superfluous question. It is not possible that I could have consented to your marriage with a poor man. In England we never do such things; we never throw our pearls away."

"No—you sell them."

"I have nothing against Stanford," he said, ignoring her remark. "Indeed, he has always seemed to me an upright and honest young fellow—a little wild, perhaps, and rough, the fault of his colonial breeding—but I cannot feel sorry for him. It was a piece of presumption on his part to look so high."

"High!" she laughed. "He little knows us."

Her father flushed angrily, but suppressing his wrath said gently, "My dear, of what use are these

J 2

angry words and recriminations ? Can Stanford save
you ? Can he raise our house from the mire ?"

"He will work for you and me; you shall never
miss your home; instead of losing a child you
shall gain one. Oh, father," she cried, falling suddenly at his knees, "you don't know how good
he is, what he has promised, and how much I love
him. Send this horrid man away; let him take
the place, sell us up—so much the better. We
shall be free of him then, free to go, to hate him,
as I know you do! Tom will protect you for the
love he bears me. He has nearly three hundred
pounds saved up. We will go away into another
part of the country, and forget this place and all
the horrid past."

Mr. Franklin held his face away from those
beseeching eyes. He had not courage enough to look
into them. They might have made him waver; and
he had dreamt of much.

"It's too late," he said. "Besides, I could not sell
my independence to—to one who had been my servant. Come, dear! Be brave and dry your pretty
eyes. I shall expect to see you in the drawing-room
presently, looking your very best. You will not dis-
appoint me ? "

"I will come."

He kissed her again and departed. But before he
returned to his guest, who was moodily pacing up and

down all this time, he stole softly to his study and imbibed a little courage. He considered that it had been a very trying interview, and that the refreshment had been honestly earned.

When Alice entered the room in which the two men were standing, Wingrove immediately stepped over to her, and taking the hand she extended carried it to his lips.

"It has seemed an eternity," he whispered. She smiled wearily in reply, and sank into a convenient chair.

If any irresolute thoughts had, for one moment, made the squatter waver in his purpose, the sight of this beautiful girl in her soft white dress, a dress all made of laces and silks—a thing that defied the ingenuity of man to describe, but which clung to her and fell about her, setting off her graceful shape to advantage—entirely banished them. Indeed, Mr. Wingrove thought he had never seen such a *bundle* of loveliness, and he felt as though he could scarcely refrain from clasping it. Yet, happy, intoxicating thought! it would soon be his, his in all its softness and its beauty, its languor and its fire; his to love and to caress, for ever *his!* There was something maddening in that thought, and as he drew near to her with devouring eyes and pulses all aglow, is it little wonder that Mr. Franklin should have slipped from the room without his knowledge?

"Miss Franklin—Alice," he said, "how beautiful you are."

She started like one awakened from a dream—an unpleasant dream.

"It is very good of you to say so."

"It is true, and therefore only natural that I should say so. There is no one in my eyes who can compare with you, and I have come to-night," he added in a low voice, "to know my fate. Are you going to make me the happiest or the most miserable of men?"

"What will make you the happiest or the most miserable?"

"Your answer."

"Mr. Wingrove," she said, "I have been perfectly candid with you all along; I have trampled on my pride; it seems to me as though I had degraded my womanhood. Yet I have been honest, have I not?"

"You have," he answered, "and I never disliked honesty before." He smiled in an undecided sort of way, wondering at the strange, firm tone her voice had taken.

"Then let us deal honestly to the end. You wish me to become your wife?"

"It is the one hope of my life."

"And yet you know that I cannot come to you with a free heart?"

"Yes, I know. Have you not told me so in your

cruel, passionless way? And yet I love you so that I can forget even that; the rest I must leave to Heaven."

She smiled scornfully at this.

"Heaven," she said, "has nothing to do with us. We had better leave it alone."

"Heaven has everything to do with you," he replied, "for you are heaven." He sank into a chair beside her as he spoke.

It is certain that if Stanford had been the author of half the sweet things which fell so glibly from this wily, this audacious politician's lips, she would have thought them sweeter than honey; but these very words, issuing from a source so hateful, so transformed them that they sounded like bitter sneers. Poor old Tom was wild and passionate, but he was true; this man she knew not how to take. She could not determine whether those words of his were the expression of a real affection, or but so many veiled sarcasms, which, while affecting admiration and humility, none the less showed the power behind. That she was in his power they both knew, and while it made one thrill with satisfaction, it drove the other to the verge of madness. Yet was she forced to listen to his advances, and when he seized her hand to let it linger. It is true he would have given much to have felt the answering pressure of her little fingers; but so that he could press them he was

content. When men of fierce and wilful natures
determine to reach an object, they care little on what
they trample, so that they gain it. And woman was
ever to be won by pressing.

Mr. Wingrove had his own ideas about the gentle
sex, and knowing that vanity is one of their prevailing
vices—as, indeed, it is of all humanity—he did all
within his power to feed that insidious flame, well
knowing that though he might not succeed in creating
a favourable impression, he could scarcely be hustled
from the shrine. From time immemorial has the
beauty of woman commanded man's highest admiration, so that she has very properly learnt its worth and
placed a prodigious value upon it; and though it may
not be for you or me, it yet is open to our admiration,
and it is ten to one that she will not think ill of us
for our reverence. Now Mr. Wingrove believed that
no woman could remain insensible to, or unaffected
by, a sustained pæan of glorification, and he exhausted
his parliamentary eloquence in praise of her loveliness.
He had taken her hand, as we have said; he would
have taken her waist next and then her lips, indeed
his right arm had advanced as far as the back of her
chair, and was contemplating with no little delight—
if an arm may be permitted to contemplate—an ex-
cursion round her form, when the door was flung
suddenly open and Mr. Franklin, bearing a bag in his
hand, appeared.

Wingrove bounded to his feet with a smothered oath, but there was no look of alarm on the intruder's face. Nay, rather it seemed to regain some of its lost dignity. There was nothing obsequious in his manner now. Even his unpleasant eyes could look straight and steadily ahead. He carried himself like a free man.

"You will pardon my interruption, Wingrove," he said, advancing with a smile, "but I have some important business to transact with you."

"Yes, yes, I'll see you presently," replied the squatter impatiently.

Mr. Franklin, however, paid no heed to this remark. Advancing to his daughter, he took her by the hand and led her to the door.

"You will pardon me, dear," he said, "but I have some business of a very important nature to transact with Mr. Wingrove. Courage!"

She looked at him, astonished beyond words, but, seeing the smile of hope on his face, passed from the room.

CHAPTER IX.

SURPRISES.

WE must go back a step or two and follow Mr.
Franklin when he slipped so quietly from the room,
leaving the squatter and his daughter in undisturbed
possession. The recollection of his own young days
appealed to him in this instance. He remembered
that lovers never appreciate the presence of a third
person. It is a most singular thing, but they do not.
With them it is not a case of the more the merrier.
Love-making is an extremely delicate process, often a
most sacred and holy one—oftener not; but it is a
process through which most people go and therefore
should command our respect. Why the outsider should
always treat love-making as a joke remains a mystery.
You may be sure it is no joke to the poor swain who
struggles between hope and fear, who is in a very
whirl of excitement, and who would as soon face a
field of artillery as those blue eyes of hers.

Seizing his opportunity, then, Mr. Franklin slipped
quietly from the room and made his way to the study,
where, sinking into one of his comfortable chairs, he
indulged in the equivocal blessing of thought. And
you may be sure his thoughts were not of the most

enviable nature, for argue in his favour as he may, he could not argue away the terrible truth that he was selling his daughter. Necessity, they say, is a stern taskmaster, and urges us to many a guilty act, but they are not such acts as this. Rather it is the evil which is in us, the slothful nature, the dread of the unseen, which is only dreadful because it is unseen. He pitied the girl with all his heart, he hated the man. A dozen times he sprang from his chair; a dozen times he fell back in it. Now he would save her from this hateful marriage, no matter what the risk, and yet that risk, that unseen monster, proved too much for his wavering heart. After all, it was better to let the affair run smoothly on. Wingrove was not a half bad sort of fellow; she at least would learn to respect him, and most probably would be proud of the reputation he was sure to build up for himself. This Stanford business was surely but a girl's fancy? She would soon see its folly, and it was much better to repent it as the wife of Martin Wingrove than as that of the ex-manager. Yet he could not altogether forget those wistful eyes, that passionate appeal, and the memory of them made him hate the man who wielded such authority.

For one who had lived his selfish life, had come and gone at his own sweet will, who had stayed not to gratify a whim or a desire, this was an almost unbearable situation, and had it not been for the agreeable companionship of a bottle of whisky, he would have flounced into that drawing-room and bade the Member depart and do his worst. Even as it was, a righteous indignation, inspired partly by the invigorating fluid, seized upon him, and he was wondering seriously if it would not become him as a father and a gentleman to put a stop to this most cruel mockery of a holy sentiment, when he heard a knock, low, hurried, impatient, at his door, and in reply to his invitation to enter who should walk in but Stanford !

"Hallo !" cried Mr. Franklin, surveying him with astonishment and annoyance, "what brings you here ?"

"May I have a drink first ?"

"Help yourself."

Stanford did as he was bidden, first laying a small bag, which he had held beneath his arm, on the table. Mr. Franklin watched him narrowly as he mixed himself the drink, and noticed that he looked very fatigued and travel-stained, and that he had evidently just returned from a long journey.

"Now, sir," cried the master of Koorabyn sharply, after his guest had refreshed himself, "may I inquire the object of this visit ? You seem to have forgotten the terms upon which we parted."

"Not at all, sir." There was a deference in the young man's tone which only the father of his adored one could have exacted after a greeting so discourteous. "I remember them only too well, and sorry I am that they ever left your lips."

"No doubt. But what has that to do with your visit, pray?"

Stanford hesitated for a moment, and then exclaimed suddenly, as though determined to plunge at once into the matter, "You must pardon me beforehand what I am going to say, for it not alone concerns you and me, but one whom we both love dearly."

"I am afraid, sir, that I cannot listen to anything of the kind."

"You must, Mr. Franklin."

"Must, eh?" he exclaimed angrily.

"Pardon me. I mean that this is a matter of the utmost importance, a matter which we neither can nor must avoid. Let us talk for a time as man to man, and forget if you can that I have in any way unwittingly annoyed you."

"Well, what is it? I suppose I must listen since you force me." He laughed as he spoke, took out a cigarette, and lit it with the most tantalising complacency.

"You, sir, know that I love Miss Franklin?"

"Really!" said her father superciliously.

"I never told you before," continued the young man, "because it was her wish that our engagement should remain secret till I was in a position to come to you and say, 'See, sir, this is what I can do for your daughter.' But in the meantime another came, a man of wealth and power—pardon me, sir, hear me out. This man was one whom she in her heart of hearts detested, but he was rich. He could command. At his bidding you turned me away, though I had served you as faithfully as one man could serve another."

"I admit the service, Stanford; I have nothing to say against that. But there was a reason, an all-powerful one, of which I could not tell you."

"I knew that too. This sword of Damocles which he held above your head was a mortgage on the run —the sum three thousand pounds, or thereabouts. Your daughter's hand was to be the price of that mortgage. Well, then, give it to me, sir; there is the money." He placed his hand on the bag as he spoke.

Mr. Franklin bounded to his feet, a look of wonder and incredulity upon his face.

"Do you mean to say that you have three thousand pounds there?" he asked.

"I have, and it is yours—for her sake."

"But, by Jove, I can't take this from you, Stanford. Where the deuce did you get three thousand pounds?"

Stanford winced slightly, but replied immediately, "I have some relations in Sydney; you know, my father was a merchant there."

"This is certainly a most generous offer, but I am not sure that I ought to avail myself of it."

"Why not?" asked Stanford anxiously. "It will clear you and save her. You must accept it, Mr. Franklin, if only for her sake."

"You seem very anxious, Mr. Stanford. Do you want to drive a bargain too?"

"A bargain!" echoed the young man. "God forgive you; don't you know that I would lay down my life for her?"

"Then suppose I accept this money?"

"You must repay me at the rate of two hundred a year."

"Fifteen years, eh?"

"Yes, fifteen years. It is not a hard bargain."

"And the interest?"

"There will be no interest."

"Stanford," said Mr. Franklin, approaching the young man with outstretched hand, a pained feeling in the eyes, a lump rising in the throat, "I am your eternal debtor. Give me your hand, boy; you are as noble as she said you were. I accept your loan and thank you a thousand times. By Jove, Wingrove shall have his walking ticket—his ticket-of-leave, as his father had before him. I hate him, damn him! You can't imagine what that brute has made me suffer these last few months. But what could I do, bound hand and foot? I have been a cur, Stanford, a fearful cur, but I couldn't part with the old place."

"And she?" asked Stanford, thinking it would be unwise to go into the why or wherefore of Mr. Franklin's actions.

"She," exclaimed her father earnestly, "is the bravest, noblest little woman in the world. To have saved the old place she would have married that brute. She's with him now, undergoing the tortures of the pit. But we'll save her, Stanford, eh?"

"God bless her!" said the young man devoutly. Mr. Franklin looked up into his face, and saw his eyes bright with unshed tears.

"He will, never fear."

There was a pause for a few moments during which Stanford walked to the other end of the room; but returning somewhat hastily he said, "I have still two conditions to impose. On no account must you breathe a word of this to Miss Franklin, for she might look upon me as one who has a right to approach her, and that, you understand, is exactly what I do not want. When I am allowed the honour of approaching her, it must be with her permission."

"If your other condition is of a similar nature," said her father, "I don't anticipate much difficulty in complying with it."

"You shall judge. When you offer this money to Wingrove you are sure to astonish him. It is ten to

one he will question you, but on no account tell him
how you got the money, most of all, do not tell him it
was I who brought it. It would also be as well to
part with him in a friendly spirit. He is a power in
these parts, and could make himself more than disagreeable—as we have seen. Tell him that you have
been trying to raise the money for months; that it
came sooner than you anticipated. You know what
I mean. Only do not let him think that you look
upon it as Miss Franklin's ransom."

"I understand and thank you. It would be
as well to smooth the brute the right way. I only
hope that I shall be able to treat him with ordinary
civility. And now about yourself. What do you
intend to do? Will you come back to me? Will you
take a share in the run?"

"Perhaps, later; but not now. Thank you all the
same. My uncle suggested that I should take a run
over to Sydney, and I'm thinking of turning up the
bush for a time."

"Why I have heard you say a score of times that
you love every blade of grass on its ugly face."

"And so I do; and every leaf and every tree, and
every breath that blows through them. But the bush,
after all, is apt to warp one's knowledge of men and
the world. Besides," he added with a smile, "I think
there is more money to be made in town."

"I am glad to see you think so well of money,

K

Stanford. It's an absolute necessity. But there's my
hand. If at any time I can be of service to you, you
may command me."

"Thank you. You will not forget my warning?"

"Not I—though I can't see why I shouldn't tell
them who the good fairy was. It would be a rare
triumph over Wingrove."

"On no account, no!" said Stanford hastily.
"It would be no triumph for me to beat such a
man."

"But Alice! she would be delighted."

"No, no; it is a whim of mine."

"Well, I suppose a man may have a whim as well
as a woman; and this mystery will add to the flavour
of the business, won't it? Reads a bit like one of
those infernal novels. But, thank heaven, it will
deliver me from the dominion of that insufferable
brute."

Then Stanford took another drop of whisky and
water, because his host would insist upon their
pledging each other, shook hands with that gentleman and departed as silently and mysteriously as he
had come.

"Now, sir," cried Wingrove turning furiously on
Mr. Franklin immediately Alice had quitted the room,
"what the deuce do you mean by such an unwarrant-
able intrusion?"

Mr. Franklin smiled amusedly. "You must pardon me, Wingrove. I assure you I waited and waited; but you lovers are so exceedingly selfish, and so very long-winded, that my patience was at last exhausted."

"By heaven!" thundered the Member, "I'll not be trifled with like this!"

"My dear Wingrove, what are you talking about? Trifle with you! What on earth do you take me for? I was never more earnest in my life. The fact is, I've had some splendid news."

"I'm very pleased to hear it," growled the squatter; "but you might have kept it to yourself for a little while longer."

"I'm awfully sorry, Wingrove—I am, upon my soul; but this is news one could not keep."

"It must be of great importance!" said the Member sneeringly.

"It is, Wingrove. It is of such moment that it has made another man of me." And he certainly looked a good ten years younger. "You don't ask what it is?" he added.

"Considering that you are dying to tell me."

"Quite right, Wingrove—quite right. Well it's this. I know that you are the best of friends and most considerate of creditors; but ever since I heard of that partner of yours, that horrible blood-sucking harpy—how you can have anything to do

with such a man surprises me!—ever since I heard
of him, and your description was not very flattering,
I have been in a state of terror. Some time ago
I wrote to an old friend of mine in Melbourne
—a man to whom I once did a good turn. You
will be pleased to know that I have just received
an answer."

Mr. Wingrove was evidently much relieved by
this vague statement, for he allowed an unconscious
sigh of satisfaction to escape him.

"Letters," he said, "are of little value in themselves."

"Letters," ejaculated Mr. Franklin in tones of
simulated astonishment. "I said nothing about
letters. I said an answer. Here it is." He held the
little bag out as he spoke.

The Member looked both puzzled and angry.
"Look here, Franklin, what are you driving at?"

"Driving at, my dear Wingrove? nothing! My
friend has relieved my necessities, that is all. This is
the relief." He patted the horrid little bag in a
tantalising sort of way.

The squatter began to look uneasy. His eyes flew
over the bag to his companion's face, then back again
to the bag.

"What is it?" he asked. "What have you
there?"

"Three thousand pounds."

"What!" cried the squatter incredulously, "three thousand pounds! You are jesting, Franklin."

"I think not; at least, such was not my intention. Look and see." He undid the bag and disclosed to the wondering eyes of the squatter packets upon packets of bank notes.

"Yes, that's money right enough," said the Member, as though to own so much was a disagreeable effort, "but from whom did you get such a sum?"

"Really, Wingrove!"

"But you did not have this an hour ago?"

"I did not. It came but a few minutes since—brought by a special messenger."

"A stranger?"

"As much as one could be who brings such credentials." But though Mr. Franklin smiled as he said these words, he had hesitated for a moment before he could reply to the squatter's simple question.

"I see. A welcome stranger, eh?" But the Member for Billabong had marked that hesitation, and had also noted the reply. "Well," he continued with a laugh, a strong effort at indifference, "it's pay up, is it? By Jove, I never expected this."

"Such is my intention. I am sorry you should have thought so poorly of me."

"Not of your wish, but your capacity."

Mr. Franklin replied somewhat loftily, "I am not yet entirely devoid of friendship," and began to hand out the bundles of notes; but Wingrove, drawing near to him, placed his hand upon his arm.

"Put them back," he said, "I don't want the money."

"But your partner?"

"Leave me to settle with him."

"I don't quite understand you."

"Then let me explain. I do not want the money, for what is a beggarly three thousand to me? but I do want your daughter."

"My daughter is her own mistress. I cannot control her choice."

"You can try. You were willing enough to do it an hour ago."

An angry taunt rose to the Englishman's lips, but he refrained from giving it utterance. "That *was* an hour ago," he said.

"Am I to understand that you will abandon me, Franklin?"

"Abandon you, my dear Wingrove, no! I respect and admire you. I have always said that you are the Coming Man, and if you are not Premier inside of two years I shall never trust my judgment again."

"Yes, yes," said the squatter impatiently, "but that is scarcely what I mean. Will you continue to use your influence with Miss Franklin for my sake? Do so, and neither you nor she shall ever regret the day that made her mine."

"In an affair of this nature, Wingrove, a father counts for nothing. I have no doubt whatever that if my daughter married you, she would do exceedingly well for herself. I hope you will be able to bring her round to my way of thinking."

"But you must aid me, Franklin."

"My dear fellow, have I not done all a man could do? I have sung your praises so that I am sure she must have sickened at the thought of so much virtue."

"Then you refuse?"

"My dear Wingrove, I refuse nothing; I remain neutral."

"Look you, Franklin, I have had your honour, reputation, life itself, in my hands for many months now. By the up-raising of a finger I could have crushed you, utterly and completely. Yet have I proved myself anything but your friend and well-wisher? What I have done for you I would do again, ay, and more. Let me have your aid in this matter, and you shall never regret it. There, there, don't answer now. Think it over a bit. If you will help me you may return that bag to your friend with thanks. If, however, you decide upon remaining neutral, you may send the money round in the morning."

When the Member for Billabong had departed,
Mr. Franklin went in search of his daughter, and
broke to her the good news of their deliverance ; and
exactly one hour after, such had been the power of
her prayers and tears, he, in company with one of his
trustiest hands, set out for Wingrove Station with the
bag of notes before him.

CHAPTER X.

HOW THE NEWS WAS RECEIVED.

In the meantime the story of the Wooroota bank robbery had been flashed from end to end of the continent, and in Melbourne especially, as being the capital of the colony in which the outrage was committed, the excitement became intense. The papers published "extraordinaries," or special editions; crowds collected round the offices of the leading journals, and every rumour was greedily devoured or widely circulated. Such daring had not been known since the extirpation of the notorious Kelly Gang, from whose book the new bushrangers had evidently taken a leaf. The public conscience was aroused, the public voice shrieked loudly. Was it possible, it asked, that our expensive police system could protect life and property no better than this? Was the country to be again disgraced by the maladministration of the Kelly days? Was the great north-eastern district to be swayed once more by a handful of desperadoes? Were life, property, liberty, all to be at the disposal of a couple of cold-blooded wretches who had failed to add murder to their other crimes simply because they had met with no opposition? This time the country must not be thrown into a state of terror. It must protect itself. Let the honest men of the district band themselves together, take their rifles in their hands and hunt the wretches down! That was the only remedy, for everyone knew the police would never take them—that is, unless like the Kellys they were fools enough to run into the lion's mouth. Oh, the poor police! How they were taunted, sneered at and jeered at; accused of every failing from cowardice downwards. And the two troopers who had actually seen and spoken to the robbers were so overwhelmed with ridicule—for everyone seems to expect a policeman to be a miraculous being—that their very presence in Wooroota was a standing disgrace to the rest of the force, and they were accordingly removed to another part of the country.

Wooroota was once more in a whirl of excitement. Strangers flocked from all parts to gaze upon the scene of the outrage ; and passengers by the various trains which plied between the two capitals always said to each other when entering its station, " This is where the great bank robbery took place." Riders, and vehicles of all descriptions, thronged the streets, and the eyes of the tradesmen danced as their brains calculated the returns. A bushranging exploit was a splendid thing for trade. Long may such heroes thrive! There was scarcely a tradesman in the place who would not have been downright sorry to have

heard of their capture. Which shows that all the
world can never be expected to see the same thing in
the same light. There were the troopers, too, legions
of them. They were met at every turn on horseback
or afoot. You would have thought it was an army
come to repel an invader, instead of being on the
look-out for a couple of thieves. But when men
"take to the bush" it is always a serious matter.
No one knows what will follow; and as the Government had more than once been bitten, it was determined to spare no effort in suppressing this latest
outbreak.

Yet the robbers had got clear away, and, what was
worse, had left no clue behind. Their trail had been
followed up according to Mr. Parsons' directions; they
found the horse and trap uninjured, but not a trace of
the culprits. As for the worthy clerk, he had rightly
foreseen his value. Like the great poet, he awoke one
morning to find himself famous. He was in such
demand for a full week after the outrage, that a
detachment of police had to protect him from the
fearfully aggressive importunities of greedy news-
collectors. He drove with the police to the spot at
which he had alighted from the bushrangers' trap;
he recounted their every word and deed, and expressed no little admiration for the excellent way in
which they had carried out their programme. Had
they not taken him unawares he would not have

yielded up the treasure without a struggle; but what
could one unarmed man do against two bloodthirsty
desperadoes ? He also made much of the conversation he held with them concerning their personality;
enlarged upon the mysterious replies of one of the
men; advocated his theory, in fact, and got many to
believe in it. People will believe in anything they
cannot comprehend.

His description of the men, however, was not calculated to elucidate the mystery which surrounded
them.   They looked like respectable bushmen, or
small farmers, he said; one wore a light tweed coat,
the other a dark one; one had on a straw hat and the
other a light felt.   He couldn't say what their trousers
were like; but they both had long dark beards, and
one had grey eyes and the other brown.   They used
no name when addressing each other—stop! When
he came to think it over he recollected that only
one of them—he with the grey eyes—had done any
talking at all; the other did nothing but chuckle,
just like an amused spectator at a play.   But he was
quite sure that the man who had done all the talking
was no common thief, for he spoke like an educated
man, and had a style of his own quite different from
the ordinary bushman. This, of course, lent a still
further zest to the affair, for the community dearly
loves to read of a lady or gentleman who has taken
the broad path ; and when that individual's name is

shrouded in mystery he or she immediately becomes an object of exceptional interest. At least, it was so in this case. Who could the mysterious bushrangers be? Some, as we have said, accepted Mr. Parsons' theory, and were quite prepared to argue that Dan Kelly and his two associates did not perish in the fire at Glenrowan; others were quite sure that the robbers had descended from that dangerous convict class which had bred so many evil doers; while others, again, were just as positive that it was the police themselves who had committed the outrage, while the more cynical few hinted that Mr. Parsons might possibly throw a little more light on the subject. It was not the first time a bank clerk had embezzled the funds. Look to it, Mr. Parsons! There are some people you cannot deceive in spite of your theories and your importance.

In the meantime messages had been sent to all the local magnates in the district, investing them with power to apprehend or detain any suspicious person or persons, and the way in which the police filled the lock-ups and prisons with inoffensive tramps, etc., was the cause of no little merriment throughout the land.

It was nearly two days after the outrage at Wooroota before the news of it reached Mr. Martin Wingrove. He saw Sergeant Jones of the Desolation police ride up the road which led to his front door, but paid little attention to the doings of that zealous officer, for he was brooding at that moment over the rebuff he had received the night before from Koorabyn. Just when he was winning too! Another moment and the girl would have been in his arms. He cursed deeply beneath his breath; and when a knock came to the door he cried out "Come in!" so savagely that had it been anyone but a sergeant of police he might have drawn back terrified.

"Well, sergeant, what do you want?"

"Official dispatch, sir," said the sergeant as he handed the magistrate—for it is in this capacity we behold Mr. Wingrove now—an official-looking document.

"So, so," he said as he hastily perused the missive, "more bushranging, sergeant, eh?"

"Yes, sir."

"What were the particulars, sergeant?"

"The Union Bank at Wooroota, sir—'stuck up' in broad daylight. They carried off between three and four thousand pounds."

The trooper then went into details, and confounded the magistrate with his record of such cool daring.

"So," said he, when the worthy officer had finished, "they wish to emulate the Kellys, do they? Well, they shall; though we'll string them all up this time."

"Can't string 'em up for robbery, sir," suggested the sergeant.

"That's a pity. Never mind, they'll pot one of you fellows before they've done. We'll hang them soon enough then."

"Thank you, sir."

"This dispatch informs me, sergeant, that they are sending us half a dozen extra men. These you must post as only you know how. Keep the country well scoured and me well informed. The Government is prepared to offer a substantial reward for the apprehension of these men; placards to that effect will be forwarded to Desolation almost immediately, and these you must have posted in every convenient place. Now then, sergeant, pull yourself together. Here is a chance to distinguish yourself. Let them see that the Desolation police are the equals of any in the force."

The sergeant saluted and withdrew.

"Strange!" muttered Wingrove, as he paced his study with a hasty step, "very strange, indeed!"

The fact is, Mr. Wingrove had racked his brains in his vain endeavour to discover how and whence Mr. Franklin really did get the money to pay him. He knew that he was hard up; he knew that if he could possibly have raised such a sum he would have done so long ago. Now, all of a sudden, this friend whom he had once befriended sends a messenger from Melbourne with a bag of money, and, hey presto! the trick is done. The idea might be feasible enough to one who knew nothing of Franklin's affairs, but to the squatter it was too ridiculous to be entertained. Who was this wonderful friend, this friend who might have let him perish months ago? How should he discover the identity of this magnanimous individual? He should like to know him. He might want to do the man a good turn one of these days.

But after the sergeant's visit an entirely new idea got into his head, and the more he thought of it the more probable it seemed. Rightly or wrongly, he now connected Koorabyn with Wooroota, and the "messenger from Melbourne" with them both. He put two and two together, bit by bit, arranging and rearranging them. Presently the edifice presented the outlines of a real thing, and he watched it with increasing pleasure. He saw, or thought he saw, the whole mystery made clear. If, as Franklin had said, a friend of his in Melbourne had sent the money, it is a thousand to one that that friend would have given him some intimation of the money being on the road. Now by the manner in which the squatter was received at Koorabyn, he felt sure that his host had no idea of the money being so near. Therefore it must have come as a surprise. This he was forced to admit, and while it exonerated Franklin from any complicity in the robbery, it made him feel all the keener on the subject of the messenger. Who was he? Once know that, and the mystery was solved. At least, so he believed.

From Wooroota to Koorabyn was between eighty
and ninety miles. The bank was "stuck up" on the
Thursday afternoon; on the Friday evening the
messenger had brought the money. This would
give that individual (always supposing that it was
he who had committed the robbery) some twenty-
six or seven hours in which to do the journey. Now
could the distance be done in that time? With a
change of horses, no doubt, if the rider were strong
enough to bear the strain; and if it should happen
to be the person on whom he had already turned his
eye, he doubted not but that he was. Yet the clerk
who had been forced to accompany the desperadoes
told of them taking the northern, or Sydney Road.
Most people had indeed believed that the men had
already crossed the border and were safe away in
some part of New South Wales. But Mr. Wingrove
did not share this opinion with them. He looked
upon the journey to the north as a blind, well
knowing that no sane men would attempt to travel
with so much money while the whole country rang
with their doings. Their game would be to lie low
till the excitement had sufficiently abated to warrant
their setting forth for more congenial climes. He
therefore scouted the idea of their having crossed
the border; and, since the wish was father to the
thought, he pictured them doubling on the clerk,
skirting Wooroota to the east or west and making

L

back in a southerly direction. It was exactly what
he himself would have done under similar circum·
stances. The idea seemed a good one; the more he
thought of it the better he liked it. It seized hold of
him and made him skip with joy. It coincided with
his every wish.

Presently he ordered his horse round, and mounting it galloped off in the direction of Mount Desolation, making certain inquiries respecting a certain
person at every house he passed. And at a little
shanty some three miles from the town he gained
the information of which he had come in search. A
certain party was seen in the bush opposite leading a
horse which appeared to be in a very weak condition.
Mr. Wingrove's heart beat strangely. He stood the
landlord a nobbler of his own vile whisky and passed
on. So, he had gained the clue; to snare the birds
could be but a matter of time. As he trotted over
the dusty road he felt himself the most important
man in the southern hemisphere.

He rode straight into the town, pulled up in
front of the Mount Desolation Hotel and called for a
drink. When the landlord saw who his customer
was, he showed him into his best parlour. It was
not often Mr. Wingrove honoured such places with
his presence, so that when he did he was received
with every consideration. But the squatter's thirst
being assuaged he prepared to go, though before he

did he asked two or three questions respecting a certain person who had lately been staying there, and learnt in answer that the person mentioned had left a week ago for Melbourne. The squatter smiled very affably as he thanked his informant and departed. He then rode over to the police camp and held an immediate interview with Sergeant Jones; and so engrossed was he with his own designs that when he emerged again he never noticed the presence of Mr. Joseph Devine on the other side of the road. But Joe had been watching him from the moment he drew rein before the Mount Desolation Hotel, and continued to watch even now he had gone. Presently he saw a trooper appear in the yard, then another; the horses were next brought from the stables and three of the officers mounted. Mr. Devine waited to see no more.

In the meantime Mr. Wingrove was speeding towards Koorabyn, his heart beating with an evil joy. If it should turn out as he hoped—and there was no reason why it should not—his revenge would be the sweetest a man had ever known. He wondered what they would say at Koorabyn when they knew. He had a surprise for Franklin, too. That worthy man little knew that when he placed those notes in the squatter's possession, he put in that man's hands a power more terrible than any he had hitherto held.

He rode up to the front gate as usual, dismounted

L 2

and made fast his horse, a thing he always did whenever he meant his visit to be a brief one. It was
customary, on these occasions, for Mr. Franklin to
implore him to send the animal to the stables, but
this time the little attention seemed to be forgotten.
The omission rather tickled the squatter. He could
laugh at the slight, considering how near his revenge
was, and how complete it would be.

Upon the verandah he was received by father and
daughter with every token of goodwill and friendship. Indeed, since she had nothing now to fear
from him she was determined to show no resentment.
She therefore smiled as affably into his face as she
did in the days when she had no suspicion of his
real intentions. And how lovely she looked! The
payment of that horrible mortgage had lifted every
sorrow from her heart. It was some time before she
could understand that she was free, free! It was like
being released from a dungeon. She danced, she
laughed, she cried. She had read of that thing called
freedom, how much men valued it, and what they
had suffered to secure it. For the first time she
seemed to understand what it meant. So must the
prisoner in his cramped cell. She plagued her father
for information respecting the advance, but in that
she suffered disappointment. He was as mute as a
graven image. Yet, what mattered it? Papa was sure
to have many wealthy friends; the only wonder was

why he had not appealed to them before. Koorabyn was their own once more, and oh, happiest of all happy thoughts, she might yet be Tom's. Poor old Tom! Why didn't he come to hear the good news? How she would scold him for staying away so long! What would he say when he knew all? Dear old · Tom! Ah, if papa could only like him a little more, how happy they might all three be! And sure enough papa was in a Christian mood that night. He acknowledged his many sins to his forgiving daughter, and even went so far as to confess that he had been inclined towards Stanford all along, and that he should never forgive himself for the wrong he had done that estimable young man. Alice thought these the sweetest words that had ever fallen from her father's lips; and ere he could speak another word she kissed him as she had never done before. That night she slept in Elysium; and this is the reason why to-day she seems so extraordinarily beautiful to the Member for Billabong.

Mr. Wingrove, as we have said, was received with courtesy by Mr. Franklin and his daughter, and if the salutations were not quite so obsequious, they were at least cordial. The squatter, however, missed the usual fuss with which he was invariably received, and being blinded by his own importance could not perceive that both Mr. and Miss Franklin wished to greet him as a friend and equal, and forget, if it were possible, the past.

"A bad business this," said he after a somewhat awkward greeting had passed between them. "You must keep a good look-out, Franklin, there's no knowing where they will turn up next."

"Where who will turn up? And what is a bad business?"

"Haven't you heard the news?"

"What news?"

"About the bushrangers."

"Bushrangers!" cried the girl with a start. Wingrove could not help smiling as he saw her glance nervously up and down the verandah, and then away out across the plains.

"No," said Mr. Franklin, "I have not. What is it?"

"A gang has just 'stuck up' the Wooroota bank and cleared out some three or four thousand pounds."

"And when was this?"

"On Thursday afternoon in broad daylight. They made the clerk fork out the money and then took him for a drive with them through the town."

"Dear me; will these outrages never cease?"

"Presumably not."

"Are the men known?"

"No."

"Have the police any clue?"

"No, sir, they have not. All that is known is that the ruffians took the Sydney Road."

"Then I suppose they are safe over the border now?"

"Do you?" asked Wingrove meaningly. "I don't."

"Why then," said Mr. Franklin, with just the slightest shade of anxiety in his tone, "do you believe they doubled, so to speak, and came south?"

"Exactly. That is the opinion I have held from the first moment I heard they had taken the Sydney Road."

"But it is a long way from here to Wooroota."

"What has that to do with it?"

Mr. Franklin dropped his eyes before Wingrove's eager look.

"I only thought," he replied, "that it would take some time for them to get this far if they intended to pay us a visit."

The squatter laughed almost harshly, and began to flick the dust from his boots with the whip he held.

"You will be prepared for them, Franklin?"

"Trust me."

"Keep your eyes open, you know. We must nip these rascals in the bud."

"That we must. But won't you come and take something?" Mr. Franklin had, in some unaccountable manner, grown exceedingly nervous during the latter part of this interview.

"No, thank you," laughed the Member, "I must

be off and set my traps for these ruffians. Pardon the joke, Franklin. It was unintentional, I assure you. My respects to you, Miss Franklin. Good-day!"

He swung down the gravel path as he spoke, his heavy crunching tread being distinctly audible till he stopped beside his horse. Unhitching it he mounted and rushed off in hot haste, and as he galloped fiercely along the dusty road he kept repeating to himself, "I've got them both! Got them both—by God!"

CHAPTER XI.

THROW YOUR HANDS UP!

A WEEK flew quickly by and yet no clue to the robbers had been found; as yet even their identity was shrouded in mystery. Give the police a clue, however slight, and their ingenuity and power will unravel it; but without that clue, not being gifted with second sight, they are but ordinary individuals. The Government had placarded the whole of the north-eastern district with descriptions of the men—culled from Mr. Parsons' rather vague statements—and also offered a reward of five hundred pounds for such information as would lead to the apprehension and conviction of the offenders. This, it is scarcely necessary to say, stimulated the troopers to extraordinary exertions; they scoured the country in all directions, leaving, as they thought, no part of it unexplored, and arresting harmless swagmen by the dozen. Of course, nothing came out of these proceedings. The men always proved to the satisfaction of the officials that they were in no way connected with the outrage, and the hopeful and ambitious trooper had to go forth again to seek for fame and fortune. Naturally, the public laughed. It always does. It knew very well

that the police would never capture these ruffians.
The dunderheads! They never did anything but
jostle decent people and arrest drunken men. Bur-
glars, murderers, bushrangers—all might run rampant
through the country! They were feared and accordingly respected; and everyone knew that the whole
force would scamper away at the sight of a loaded
rifle. Yet the force did its duty despite the sneers
and jeers of an irritated public, but the Wooroota
bank robbery remained as great a mystery as
ever.

To one man, however, the affair was not so great a
mystery as it appeared to the rest of the world. Like
a bloodhound he had scented the trail, and with
untiring energy pursued it. He knew he was on the
right track; indeed, he had never doubted it for a
moment. Not that he was cleverer than the rest of
his species, only that he knew more. He had a bag
of bank-notes in his safe which solved as plainly as
written words the great mystery. Mystery! He
laughed aloud as he thought of it. Here was the
whole of Australia in a ferment over the identity of
the robbers, and he had his hand almost on the chief
culprit's shoulder. We say almost, for though that
hand was outstretched the shoulder was not beneath
it. This fact caused the squatter just a little uneasiness. He had two troopers watching Koorabyn day
and night. No one came, no one went; nothing was

done of which he did not know every particular. Yet that one shoulder came not beneath his grasp, and as the days flew on and ran themselves into a week, Mr. Wingrove's uneasiness turned to positive anxiety. The individual on whom he had set his eye, and on whom he longed to set a pair of handcuffs, had not been seen or heard of for six full days. Yet for reasons, which may be apparent, he trusted in his knowledge of human nature; sat down and waited.

It was a week, as we have said, since the great robbery; no news of the desperadoes had been obtained, and as public interest is a thing which must be fed to live, the dearth of incidents had almost starved the monster; it howled occasionally, but was' quickly relapsing into indifference. Even Miss Franklin had sufficiently recovered from the terrifying thought of bushrangers to resume her equestrian exercises, and on this particular day she might have been seen once more careering across the plains on the back of that equine marvel, Boomerang. According to his mistress, who was no poor judge of horseflesh, Boomerang was the noblest, swiftest and best four-footed creature that was ever foaled in the district. Give him the short springy grass beneath him, let go his head, and if there was an arrow after him he would outstrip it. Then see him clear creek, or fallen trunk, or fence of wire or rails! A slight pressure on the bit and he

rose to it like a bird; a thud as he struck the turf
on the other side, and then, gathering up his strength,
as it were, away he sailed again. Oh, those glorious
rides in the morning while the dew yet lay on
the grass, and the sun, no warmer than the blush on
the young girl's face, filled the forest with awakening life. Or a gallop over the parched earth after
a heavy shower when the very dust exhales the
sweetest of perfumes. On such occasions as these
Alice would forget the whole world and live only
in the enjoyment of the moment—she and Boomerang. They understood each other well; at the
sound of her voice the great horse would bound
along as though revelling in the enjoyment it gave
its mistress.

To-day it was fresher than usual, for it had not
been out for a week, and as she turned its head towards Mount Desolation, it set off at a long striding
gallop which soon brought the outlines of that mountain within easy range of the eyes. Yet on she sped,
thinking neither of horse nor distance, but of Stanford,
and why he had not been near her for so long. She
was free now; free to take his hand, look up into his
eyes and say, "I am yours, Tom—take me." Of
course he did not know the good news; how should
he? What a glorious surprise it would be for him,
dear old fellow, and her heart glowed at the thought
of his happiness.

Just at that moment a solitary horseman dashed round the bend of the road ahead of her. She involuntarily drew rein, for the thought of the horrid bushrangers immediately beset her. But in a few moments she was relieved of all anxiety, for in the rider she recognised the subject of her thoughts.

"Oh, how you frightened me," she cried, as soon as he came up. "I thought you were one of those horrid bushrangers."

He laughed oddly, stooping to adjust his stirrup strap as he did so. "Did you? And if I had been, what would you have done?"

"Screamed, I suppose," she laughed. "But you scarce look yourself, Tom. Are you, have you been ill?"

"Not in the least. Why do you ask?"

"You look—I'm sure I can't describe your looks, but you have changed, somehow, and you are quite old."

"Well, am I not getting old?"

"Age is always a joke to twenty-seven. But, truant, where have you been all this time?"

"Has it seemed long?"

"Long," she repeated. "Has it not seemed long to you?"

"An eternity," he answered seriously.

"Then why did you stay away?"

"I—I thought it might be better, Allie."

"Ah, you foolish old boy."

"I am, dearest, but I love you."

She turned a happy face to him. His own gloomy looks quite startled her.

"Is anything the matter, Tom ?"

He started. "No, no. Why do you ask ?"

"You look, seem so strange. One would think something dreadful were going to happen."

"Perhaps it is," he answered moodily.

She luckily misunderstood his meaning, and answered with a smile, "Nothing can happen now. Father has paid the mortgage—and I am free."

Strange to say, he did not show any of that delight which she had pictured.

"I am glad of that," was all he said.

Her face fell.

"I should have thought you would have been more than glad," she answered somewhat petulantly, and, giving Boomerang a sudden cut across the shoulder, darted from him. But he was soon beside her again.

"Of course I am more than glad, Allie. Anything that gives you joy commands my adoration. You know what you are to me, dear. Whatever I have been or may be, you must never forget that I love you with all the power that is in me." He brought his horse still closer to hers, put out his arm, seized her and kissed her. "And now," he continued, "tell me all the news, and all about this good fairy."

" I cannot tell you of him," she replied, "because papa, for some reason or other, refuses to disclose his name. But this much I do know, that he is a friend of papa's, that he lives in Melbourne, and that he is awfully rich. Papa might have applied to him before, you know, but poor papa is proud, and could not stoop to beg."

" I suppose not. He would rather sell his daughter," he muttered to himself.

" Mr. Wingrove was there when the money came. A special messenger brought it all the way from Melbourne. Was it not kind and thoughtful of papa's friend ?"

" Very. And so Wingrove was there at the time ? "

" Yes." She blushed scarlet at the recollection.

" Did he see the messenger ? "

" Oh, no."

" Are you sure of that ? "

" How could he—when I was with him ? Had he seen the man I must have seen him too. But what would it have mattered if he had ? "

" Nothing, of course. And how did he take the news ?"

" Very ungraciously."

"I expect so. Well, thank heaven, that difficulty is done with. You are free of him at last. Your father can once more call Koorabyn his own. What is there now to prevent our marriage?"

"Nothing." Her eyes dropped modestly as she said the word.

He pressed her to him, kissing her like one half mad.

"Your father?" he asked.

"Papa is your friend now, dear—he always was. It was Mr. Wingrove who was your enemy."

"I know it. And you think your father would give his consent to our marriage now?"

"Yes."

"Then let me tell you of a plan I have arranged. I have been thinking seriously of leaving these parts —of going to Sydney, in fact. There I may be able to improve my condition, and provide for you a fitting home."

"But why go to Sydney? Papa says that he is quite willing to take you into partnership. And you love the old place, Tom, surely?"

"I shall always remember it with feelings of reverence," he replied, looking earnestly at her, "but I think it would be better for me if I carried out my original intention. There is more scope for a man in a big town, and I want to do something more than round up cattle and sheep all my days. You would come to me there, would you not ? "

" Yes, dear, to the end of the world."

They here turned off from the main road and proceeded along a bush track which led down to the river Warrigal; here also was the southern boundary of Mr. Franklin's run. The lovers had both dismounted, and Stanford led the two horses with one hand, while with the other he drew his companion so close to him that at times she found it extremely difficult to walk, and had to tell him so.

" Very well, then," he said, " I'll carry you;" but as she objected to this, he informed her that there was a big tree down by the river. Should they go there and sit and talk ? Would he promise to behave himself? He would be as good as gold, he replied.

Knowing every inch of the ground about here, he led her to the fallen giant in question, having first made the horses fast to a couple of trees. It was a long white gum tree, without bark, smoothed and polished by wind and sun.

As they approached she might have seen his face pale as his eyes encountered a white bill which was posted on the tree, had her own not caught sight of the object at the same moment.

" Look ! " she cried, " here's another of those bills about the bushrangers—the men who 'stuck up' the

M

Wooroota bank. They're all over the place, like the bills of a circus. I hope they'll soon be caught, don't you?"

"Why should you care whether they are caught or not?"

"Why shouldn't I? One never knows when they may come and burn one out. Then bushrangers are such dreadful creatures. They do such horrible things, you know; they are always so bloodthirsty, so cruel. And—and this is the first time I have dared to come out since the ruffians have been at large."

"They will not harm you, Allie."

"I don't know. Such wicked men are equal to anything."

"Perhaps they are not so bad as you think. I grant you they are thieves, that they 'stuck up' the Wooroota bank, but they may not be so very bad for all that. The world only judges a thing by its result; it knows nothing of the fate or destiny which may have prompted these men to do what they did. And after all, what is the horrible thing they have done? They have injured no one."

"They have defied and outraged the law."

"So the newspapers say. But suppose by so doing they had relieved the necessities of those nearest to them, had raised them from hopelessness to hope, from misery to joy, what would you say then?"

"Oh, Tom, you cannot defend such people."

"I can think of them without repugnance till I know they do not deserve my sympathy. They may be a couple of poor wretches so very miserable that even the world, if it only knew their secrets, might pity them."

"But how they must have terrified that poor bank clerk; and only fancy, taking him away under the eyes of the two troopers! Mr. Wilson, who called on papa the other day, laughed so loudly when they spoke about it that he nearly had a fit. And do you know, Tom, though I am dreadfully afraid of them, I can't help admiring their boldness."

"There is nothing much to admire in them," he said.

"Perhaps not, for they, no doubt, are very low creatures; though the clerk did say that the leader of the two appeared to be a gentleman."

"The clerk was evidently little acquainted with the species."

"I suppose so; but I can't help admiring those two men, and I am sure lots of others do; but there, I'm afraid I'm very wicked, for I was awfully sorry when the Kellys were taken."

"The Kellys were murderers — these men are merely thieves. Yet you said just now that you hoped they would soon be taken."

"Well, isn't that the right thing to say, dear? Is

M 2

it not the duty of every honest man to sweep such pests from the face of the earth ? "

She was quoting the fiery articles in the newspapers ; Stanford flinched as though he had received a sharp cut from a whip.

" Never mind them, dear. They are but poor wretches at the best, who deserve your sympathy more than your anger. They will no doubt receive their punishment in due time."

" Oh, yes. Everybody says they are sure to be taken."

" I suppose so. The police swarm the country like a plague of locusts."

" Life and property must be preserved, you know. Mr. Wingrove says it means a life sentence when they are caught."

" He is very energetic, is he not ? "

" Extremely so. He has left no stone unturned to assure their capture. Only yesterday he rode over to Koorabyn and told papa all the latest movements of the police. Do you know he declares the men are not two hundred miles from Wooroota ; that he believes they are in the mountains somewhere about here, and that he will soon lay them by the heels, as he calls it ? "

" Wingrove is a very determined man. Oh, by the bye, does he ever speak of me now ? "

" Always. One of the first questions he asks when

he comes is have we seen Stanford yet? I think he has forgiven you, though. Perhaps he is not quite so bad as we imagine."

"Perhaps not."

Just then Stanford started to his feet with a sudden bound, looking to right and left with a strange eagerness. From the other side of the river came the cry of a curlew.

"I must be going, Alice," he said suddenly and excitedly. "To-morrow afternoon, at this place, I'll——" He stopped short, for again the warning cry came over the water. A third time it sounded, quickly, shrilly. There was no time to lose.

The girl had heard it too, and, recognising the familiar signal, turned to him a look of terror and wonder.

"What is it, Tom?"

Stanford seized her in his arms and kissed her eagerly.

"Nothing. Don't speak of this, dear. Tell no one we have met. Remember—to-morrow!"

He bounded from her side and sprang towards the little clump of trees in which he had tethered the horses, but ere he reached it two troopers stepped forward with uplifted rifles and barred the way.

"Surrender, Tom Stanford! Up with your hands or you're a dead man!"

He stood irresolute for a moment, looking straight

into the muzzles of the rifles. At that moment the same weird cry rang through the air; then all was still. Stanford shivered. It sounded like the wail of a lost soul.

"Come, up with your hands, Tom; the game's up."

A fierce scowl passed over Stanford's pale face. He thought of rushing on the men and making a bid for liberty. It would be that or death. The rifles were sighted with deadly precision. After all, it were wiser to surrender. All this reflection cost him but a moment. With a laugh he held his hands up high above his head. The next moment the hand-cuffs were slipped over his wrists.

He turned to the troopers with a ghastly smile. "What does this mean, sergeant?" The trooper addressed was our old friend Sergeant Jones.

"It means, Tom," replied the sergeant, who knew him well, "that you are arrested on suspicion of being concerned in the great bank robbery at Wooroota."

"But this is sheer nonsense, sergeant."

The sergeant smiled grimly. "Indeed, I hope so, Tom, though me and Tim here would split five hundred between us. Anyway," he added, "it's nothing to do with me. I only obey orders."

They then began a careful search of Stanford's person, and while employed in this duty Alice advanced to where the trio stood, her face as white as a dead woman's—her whole demeanour denoting anguish of the most terrible nature.

"Tom," she gasped, "what does this mean?"

She put out her hands to touch him, but the sergeant moved her back.

"Stand back, Miss, please. You must not touch the prisoner."

"Prisoner!"

"Tim," cried the sergeant to his companion, "fetch up Miss Franklin's horse. Pardon me, Miss," he added, as softly as so rough a voice would permit, "but you had better go home."

She, however, heeded him not. Turning to Stanford with an imploring look she said, "Tell them that they are in the wrong, dear; that you are innocent of this awful charge."

He met her tearful eyes with a faltering look. "Of course they are wrong," he said. "It is all a mistake; but they are only doing their duty and—and you had better go, dear."

"But they have no right to arrest you like this. By whose authority is it done?"

"Mr. Wingrove's, Miss. Here is the warrant."

"Ah!" The sigh escaped Stanford's lips before he was aware of it.

"It is monstrous," she cried, "monstrous!" And, being powerless to help, she burst into a torrent of tears.

Unseen by her Stanford gave the sergeant an imploring look.

"Come, Miss," said the trooper kindly, "here is your horse, let me help you to mount it. I have no doubt that Mr. Stanford is innocent of this charge. He has only to prove an *alibi*, which he of course can easily do, and then he's free again. We, you understand, are only doing our duty. The incident is unpleasant, but it's sure to end all right."

"Go, dear," urged Tom. "Trust me to prove my innocence."

She would have thrown herself in his arms and declared her trust in him had it not been for those stern men in uniform ; as it was, she bowed her head and suffered the sergeant to lend his hand. She seized the reins in a listless manner, but the good horse Boomerang required no guidance. It slowly retraced the path which led back to the main road; its mistress sat loosely in the saddle like one in a dream.

The three men watched that sorrowful form depart, and when at length the trees hid her from sight, Stanford exclaimed, "Thank God, she's gone. Now, sergeant, I am ready."

They first of all helped Stanford to mount his own horse ; then the sergeant unwound a long piece of rope which hung at his saddle, and cutting this in two, he with one half tied Stanford's feet below the belly of the horse, and with the other portion made fast his own animal to that of the prisoner.

"I think that's all," he said as he surveyed his work with a critical eye. "Does it hurt you, Tom?"

"Not in the least."

The sergeant then gave the word "forward," and the little cavalcade set out towards the town of Mount Desolation.

In the meantime Alice had awakened from her lethargy, and stung almost to madness by the terrible suspicion which now haunted her, she whipped Boomerang into a furious gallop. Arriving at the homestead she slipped from the saddle, leaving the animal to find its own way to the stable, and rushed into the study where sat her father in one of his easy armchairs with a cigar in his mouth and a book before him.

"Father," she cried, pale, excited, almost breathless, the word coming from her lips like a gasp, "who, —who was the messenger?" She leant forward on table as she spoke, as if for support.

"The messenger?" he asked.

"Yes, yes—he who brought you the money last week?"

"Really," began Mr. Franklin, "you have a most singular way of entering a room; and as for your manner of putting a question, and one too that does not concern you——"

"But it does concern me," she cried. "Father, this is no time for hesitation. Tell me, for God's sake tell me—was it Tom Stanford?"

"Well, since the secret's out, it was Tom Stanford; and a very noble fellow he is."

But his daughter heard no syllable of this encomium. With a strange, gasping cry she fell senseless at his feet.

CHAPTER XII.

FOR HER DEAR SAKE.

IT was quite dark when Stanford and his captors rode
into the police camp of Mount Desolation, so that the
officers were enabled to cage their bird unknown to the
residents of that flourishing township. Had they but
guessed that the Wooroota bushranger was in their
midst, it is safe to say there would have been little
sleep that night, at least for the adults; and had they
also known that the mysterious and notorious personage was no other than Tom Stanford, the man whom
they all knew and esteemed so profoundly, it is ten to
one they would have rushed up and opened his prison
doors. But being in utter ignorance of his presence
or arrest, they drank their beer, smoked their pipes,
and tumbled off to bed in their uneventful way.

But when Sergeant Jones had seen his prisoner
safely manacled, and had taken the double precaution
of pocketing the keys of the inner and outer doors, he
remounted his horse and set off in the direction of
Wingrove Station. He saw, as he rode up, a light
burning in the Member's study, and with an unusual
amount of assurance knocked loudly at the front door.
Orders had evidently been given to admit him at all

times, for he was shown without a word into the presence of the great man.

"Well, sergeant, any news?" asked Mr. Wingrove as he looked up from his great attack on the Government.

"We've got him, sir."

Wingrove bounded from his seat, an excited, happy flush suffusing his face. "Got him, eh? The right one, sergeant?"

"Thomas Stanford, sir."

"Ah! And where was this, sergeant?" Mr. Wingrove began to pace the room. He was much too excited to sit still.

"Down by the Warrigal—outside Koorabyn."

"I know. Was he alone?"

"No, sir. Miss Franklin was with him."

"It was a wise thought of mine to watch her."

"You ought to be in the force, sir." This was intended by the sergeant as a great compliment, and as such was received by the squatter.

"Did she—did Miss Franklin see him arrested?"

"Ay, sir, and carried on dreadful, poor thing Sobbed like a baby—as though her heart would break. I never felt a bigger blackguard in my life than when I did that job."

"You are rather too soft-hearted, sergeant," said the squatter sneeringly.

"I don't know that I'm that altogether," replied

the man somewhat tartly, " but it makes me feel queer
all the same when I see a woman blubbing. I've put
the darbies on some queer ones in my day, and I've
heard the Kellys' bullets sing alongside of my ear;
but I never could stand crying women, sir. I'd rather
face Dan Morgan with his back up than lay my hand
on a woman's shoulder and tell her she was 'wanted.'"

"I appreciate your delicacy, sergeant," said the
squatter in the same meaning tone, "and am extremely
pleased to find that your rough calling has not robbed
you of all tenderness. It is always a pity when men
forget that they are human and act the brute. But
the business in which we are now engaged will, unfortunately, admit of no generosity or fine sentiment.
You have in your keeping an exceedingly dangerous
person, and one little error might confound us both.
If you have any scruples in this affair, you know——"

" Sir, I am not a fool."

" Far from it, I am sure, my dear sergeant. You
captured him very cleverly, and in a few days
Sergeant Jones will be the hero of the hour. You
must, therefore, redouble your assiduity, sergeant, or,
if you think it necessary, I will order you an escort to
convey him to Wooroota. An escape now, sergeant,
would prove a disaster of the greatest magnitude."

The sergeant laughed loudly. " Lord," he said, " a
handcuffed prisoner strapped to his horse escape!
What do you take me for?"

"Remember, he had an accomplice."

"You are supposing now that we have got hold of the right man."

"I *know* we have. I am as certain of it as I am that I breathe. Believe me, sergeant, I know more of this affair than any man in the country."

"You certainly seem to have got hold of something that didn't come from the Commissioner."

"The Commissioner! Bah! a puppy who knows nothing but how to play cards, drink brandies-and-sodas, and hang about women. Pitchforked in by influence, he knows no more of police affairs than a wombat. Wait till I——I mean if I ever become Premier, sergeant, I'll make a few of those fellows skip, I know. But, in the meantime, let me assure you that Mr. Thomas Stanford is the right person; and let me impress upon you the vastness of this responsibility."

Sergeant Jones laughed disdainfully. "Why, bless you, sir, what's a bushranger more than an ordinary thief once you've got the tinklers on him?"

"As you please, sergeant. Though, if you say the word, there's an escort for you."

"Tim and me'll manage it, thank you, sir."

"Very well, then. Remember, when Mr. Thomas Stanford is convicted, you must come to me. I will double the reward."

"A thousand pounds!"

"Yes, sergeant, the job is worth a thousand pounds, and, unless you display that reckless generosity of yours, you need say nothing to Tim about a certain five hundred which is not on the Government proclamation."

The sergeant took an inward oath that he would not.

"But don't you really think," continued the squatter roguishly—he was so pleased with the news the trooper had brought him that he beamed all over —"don't you think that I had better send to Euraya for a couple of extra men?"

"No, sir, if me and Tim can't take him there we'll die on the road. But to satisfy you, I'll take another from Euraya to see us as far as Wooroota. Once in Wooroota Gaol"—he stopped and smiled significantly.

"Exactly. When shall you start?"

"In the morning, sir. It's fifty miles to Euraya. We shall reach it long before nightfall."

"Very well, sergeant, you know best. Only be very careful."

"A poor man with five children does not get this chance every day."

"He does not. Good-night."

"Good-night, sir." The sergeant saluted in military fashion and showed himself to the door.

Mr. Wingrove listened to the rapid strokes of the trooper's horse as they died away in the distance, and then, rising from his seat, with a cruel smile, he began to pace the room excitedly. So, the game was his at last. Stanford in the hands of the police, charged with a crime which might mean the life sentence, for the law could never be accused of leniency towards armed robbers; the girl bowed down with shame and misery; the father at his mercy, now more than ever, for he would use those bank notes yet to some purpose. What was there now to prevent him bringing these people once more to his feet? And he would, he would! He swore a terrible oath to it. They had trifled with him long enough. His turn was come now, and he would grind them beneath his heel! He ground his feet savagely into the carpet as he walked, for in imagination he was trampling on his victims, and the operation was exceedingly pleasant. Their laugh of triumph should be changed to wailing; their look of victory to one of horror. And the worst was yet to come! He laughed aloud as he pictured the capture of Stanford, and only regretted that he had not offered some resistance, that he had not shot one of the troopers down. It would have been a hanging matter then; death without a hope of mercy. And it could so easily have been. Yet, he doubted even if that was equal to the life sentence. It was a short shrift in one case, and then all was over; but the life sentence was a living death—death without oblivion.

Yes, he would like to have seen that capture;

would liked to have looked in Stanford's face and
said, " It is I who have brought you to this. Now we
are quits, you dog!" But though that pleasure was
denied him he conjured up the scene in his memory,
and embellished it with numerous incidents of his
own creation. So, he was captured in her arms? He
wondered how she would feel if this came to the
knowledge of the public. And yet this was but an
insignificant part of an ignoble whole. What would
she say if he were to tell her that her father was an
accessory to the crime; that he knew well from
whence the money had come, and that the doors of
the prison were yawning for him as well as her
abandoned lover? His white eyes shone malevolently
as he pictured these awful thoughts. A dangerous
man was Mr. Wingrove. We are sorely afraid that he
will never be Premier.

In the meantime Stanford, heavily chained, lay in
the lock-up at Mount Desolation, a prey to horror
and despair. He knew that he had done wrong, and
that justice, or what men call by that heavenly
quality, would sooner or later overtake him; but to
be trapped in sight of her, to be taken almost from
her arms, exceeded even the horror of his own vivid
brain pictures. What would she think of him? He
knew she would not believe him guilty, unless he
spoke the words from his own lips; yet the stigma
that would attach itself to his name would blight

N

her life for ever. Or, perhaps, she would never know
that he had sinned for her sake, and the dignity of her
nature might revolt against the depravity of his. He
hoped it might be so. There would then be a chance
of peace for her—and him. Her ignorance would
admit of her forgetting, and, perhaps, of courting
happiness at no distant date ; while the knowledge
that he had done so much for her sake might enable
him to look the day in the face, even through prison
bars. What would she think of him ? The newspapers would soon teem with his capture, and every
petty incident of his life would be flashed from end
to end of the continent. Then in due time would
come the fearful ordeal of a public trial. If he could
only avoid that ; if they would only take him away
somewhere and hide him. And what a mockery was
this trial ! Was he not already judged ? Yet the form
must be gone through, and he must suffer it—it was
a part of his penance.

What would she think of him ? This was the all-
prevailing thought. Would she ever know that he
had sinned for her sake ? Perhaps not. Even if she
did, might that lessen her antipathy to the felon ? A
felon ! Yes, that is what he would be—a thing from
which every honest person shrinks. Yet he had saved
her, and come what might, he had that one fair
thought to cheer him through the dreary days of the
future. It would dawn by-and-by, black and lowering

like the brow of night. They would put him away, perhaps for life. For life! What horror those two words contained. He sprang to his feet and tugged wildly, breathlessly, at his chains. He trampled on them, beat them wildly on the floor; tugged with a giant's strength to loosen the great staples from the beams, but all to no purpose. The paroxysm passed and left him gasping on his back. For life, ay! They would call it bushranging, armed robbery, and for that crime no punishment, short of death, was too severe. They could not take his life—he almost wished they might—but they could bury him alive, shut him out from the free world till his days were numbered. Well, let them— he had saved her, she was free! He would bear the punishment of a dozen lives so that she were spared all pain. He grew almost resigned to the dreadful prospect, and staring up into the dark pictured it with fantastic shapes.

Suddenly, however, he arose in a kneeling attitude, his body stiffened, he leant forward as if listening. The cry of a curlew had floated in through his grated window. His heart beat wildly, his pulses throbbed. Again came the weird cry, and yet once more, three times in all. It was the old signal.

"Joe!"

The word escaped him unconsciously. He would have answered the signal had he dared. The long night

N 2

was not yet come; the jaws of the prison were not yet locked upon him. Away in the far east there was the faintest glimmer of dawn, the palest ray of hope. He stretched out his hand and took the food which they had brought him. He would eat; he might need his strength on the morrow. Then, having refreshed himself, he lay back with a hopeful sigh, and a few minutes later he was soundly sleeping.

But on her bed in Koorabyn a young girl tossed restlessly all through that terrible night, and when they came to her next morning they found her still undressed and moaning incoherently. Her face was flushed and burning, her lips were like two streaks of fire. She looked at them with burning, bloodshot eyes, but knew no one, not even her father. They spoke to her gently, kindly, but the only sound she uttered was the heart-broken moan, "Tom! Tom! Tom!"

CHAPTER XIII.

THE SQUATTER GOES VISITING.

ON the morning following Stanford's arrest, Mr. Martin Wingrove, the respected Member for Billabong, arose exceedingly early, long before sunrise, and proceeding to his stable saddled his favourite horse and galloped off in the direction of Mount Desolation. He had spent a few hours of uneasy slumber that night, uneasy because he could not sleep, not that he suffered. On the contrary, it was the excess of satisfaction with which he surveyed the doings of the last few hours which so completely robbed him of the presence of the sweet comforter. His triumph had been greater than even he had hoped, and he had not finished yet. The father was his, and the girl should kneel to him; kneel to him with tears, implore his pity, his protection. And with Stanford gone, who was there left to thwart him? Then a wild longing to see that unhappy young man, see him in all his shame and misery, seized hold upon the squatter. What a splendid prologue to the still more splendid acts to follow. He could not rid himself of the idea. It haunted him; it made him quiver with excitement. He heard the clock in the next room strike four, and bounding from his bed pulled back the blinds. The sun had not yet risen, but it was daylight. In five minutes he was dressed, in another five he had saddled his horse—a big, powerful creature with a coat like black satin—and was away.

He heeded not the beauty of the morning, the thousand perfumes of awakening day, but galloped resolutely on. At last the town loomed in view, and as he rode into the police-yard he beheld the estimable Sergeant Jones crossing over to the stables. Beckoning to him he explained in a few words the object of his visit.

"Morning, sergeant."

"Morning, sir."

"Bird safe, eh ? "

"Well, the lock-up ain't gone, sir, so I suppose he is."

"I would like to see him, sergeant. There are a few questions I should like to put to him—officially, you understand ? "

"Then come this way, sir. You may do the interviewing while Tim and me get the horses out."

The sergeant led the Member across the yard to the lock-up, a low, square building constructed of entire logs cut so as to fit into each other at the corners: a substantial log hut, nothing more nor less. Here the officer produced a large key and undid the great door disclosing a passage with a narrow grated window at its further end through which stole light and air. On each side of this passage there were three doors, making six in all, all heavily barred and padlocked. These were the cells, and, though not many in number, were invariably capable of accommodating the criminal population—except on race weeks. Then, it is true, the drunkards and the rogues did tax the capacity of the place, but as the races were only once a year this overcrowding was looked upon as a little diversion.

The officer stopped before the farthest cell on the right hand side and immediately began to unlock it —somewhat nervously, it seemed. Yet when the heavy door swung back and he saw the prisoner rise from the blanket on which he had been sleeping, he breathed an inward sigh of relief.

" This way, sir."

" Thank you, sergeant ; you may leave us."

" I will be back in five minutes, sir."

" Very well."

The trooper went out, locking the big door behind him. The squatter advanced to the threshold of the cell, and leaning against the door, calmly surveyed the chained occupant. Through the grated window the day was already streaming, throwing its rays full in the corner where lay the unhappy prisoner. A sudden, angry look passed between them, and then Stanford turned his head away. Wingrove laughed, though for a time he uttered no word. Yet the prisoner felt those white eyes burning through him.

"So, Mr. Stanford, it's come to this, has it? You thought to master me, and here I find you on the road to penal servitude. To penal servitude, do you hear?" repeated the squatter with a harsh laugh— "to gaol for life."

"I wonder you are not ashamed to mention the word gaol."

Wingrove flushed angrily. "Ashamed or not," he said, "I have the pull of you, you dog. Do you know who has done all this, who has hunted you down, who has brought you here, who will send you to the quarries?"

"I know who will try to do so."

"Try," he laughed. "And you're as good as sentenced already."

"Indeed, and for what; pray?"

"For robbing the Wooroota bank."

Stanford laughed. "Who is going to prove it?"

"I."

"You!" disdainfully.

"Yes, I, for I have identified the messenger who brought old Franklin his ransom. Why don't you laugh now, Mr. Stanford?"

"If I were free for five minutes——" began Tom, clutching his irons.

"Free," laughed the squatter, "you will never be

free again. The law never looks with a lenient eye on the bushranger."

" Is this all you have come to tell me ? "

" Not quite. There were many reasons why I came, chief among them being the satisfaction of seeing you thus. It is a feast for me, Stanford, one which I would not willingly have missed. I told you you would rue the day you made an enemy of me ; see how I have kept my word. They'll take you from here to prison, and you'll lead a dog's life till you die, and they'll bury you like a dog when you're dead, and you may thank me for it all."

" If this is all you have to say, you may go."

" I shall be going presently—to Koorabyn. I have some business there. Shall I leave a message for poor Alice ? "

" Silence," cried Stanford, " how dare you speak of her ! "

" Oh, come," sneered the squatter, " don't you think that just a little absurd ? With you away, my dear fellow, the girl's as good as mine."

" She will never be that, thank God."

"She shall be mine as sure as there's a God in heaven. Listen to me. The money you stole from the Wooroota bank paid off the mortgage, certainly, but that, instead of freeing them, has bound them closer to me. You look bewildered ; you don't quite understand me?"

" I do not."

"Then let me explain, because I should like you to be clear on this point ; it will comfort you so by-and-by. I can prove, to the satisfaction of any thickheaded jury, that Franklin knew from whence that money came which ransomed him, that he was an accessory to the fact."

" But if you know as much as you pretend, you know this to be an infamous lie."

" I know exactly what it suits me to know—no more, no less."

" You are an abominable scoundrel ! "

Wingrove laughed harshly. " I have been one too many for you, anyway ; and Franklin too, curse him, the infernal upstart ! But I repeat, for your especial benefit, Mr. Stanford, that I know just as much as I wish to know, and that a word from me will place our Alice's father in the dock beside you."

" You must be mad ! "

" Perhaps so. But you will not deny that you had an accomplice when you 'stuck up' the Wooroota bank ? "

" Did I 'stick up' the Wooroota bank ? "

" We will suppose you did—just for the sake of argument. Shall I tell you who that accomplice was ? "

" Considering he is my accomplice, that is hardly necessary."

"Yet we may as well be clear on the subject. It was the master of Koorabyn."

Stanford gave a start which did not escape the searching eyes of the squatter.

"Oh, was it?" he said.

Wingrove had overshot the mark, had fired and failed. After carefully leading up to this point he had hoped for a fierce denial or tacit acknowledgment of the correctness of his charge, but the simple query had quite confounded him. Still, he would not let the prisoner see he entertained a thought of failure; indeed, he doubted if he had failed, for that sudden start of Stanford's told a welcome tale to the eyes that looked for it.

"It was," he replied, "and one word from me will land him by your side. And, by heaven! he shall stand there if he thwarts me again. I have him in my power, the puppy, and I'll run him to earth as I have run you—unless——"

"Unless—" repeated Stanford in spite of himself.

"Well, you know," he said with a coarse laugh, "I love Miss Franklin."

"You—love!"

"Yes, I love, or desire, or hate!—I don't know which it is, nor ever shall till I get her, and get her I will. You must think over this, Stanford," he said laughingly; "it will be something for you to do when you get a bit tired of solitude."

What Tom might have said in reply, or how much longer this interview might have lasted, it would be difficult to say, but just at that moment the great bolts on the outer door were pushed back and the sergeant appeared intimating that it was time the conversation ended. Wingrove turned from the cell with a laugh and a mock good-bye. His eyes had feasted on the degradation of his rival; his tongue had further poisoned his peace of mind. There was nothing for him now but to watch the trial and wait for the sentence of the court.

"Sergeant," he cried in a voice loud enough to be heard by the prisoner, "take good care of that infernal rascal, and if he attempts to escape don't hesitate to put a bullet through him." Then, after a few more words of warning and instructions, he remounted his big horse and rode back to breakfast.

After he had done full justice to that substantial meal—for the exercise and interview had somewhat whetted his appetite, he dressed himself with a nicer scrupulousness, and calling for another horse mounted and turned towards Koorabyn. He had made up his mind that Mr. Franklin had been Stanford's silent accomplice in the now notorious exploit at Wooroota, and he was determined to bring that irresolute being once more to his feet. He was well aware that he had no absolute, no incontestable proof of Franklin's complicity in the outrage; but that he had proof enough to command an investigation he knew well. There was the bag of notes produced immediately after Stanford's departure from the house; his refusal to state the name of the person who had lent him the money; and there were also many other little things which he had noted at different times, which all pointed to an undoubted understanding between the two men. And even if his surmises should prove false, if Franklin was entirely innocent of any offence, it would take no little trouble and no less degradation to prove it. His own course was clear. As a magistrate and good citizen it was his duty to work for the public good, and in the accomplishment of that task spare neither friend nor foe. One may find a thousand excuses for the friend who has made a slip, but for the criminal the law must speak.

These were a few of the agreeable thoughts which throbbed through the squatter's brain as he galloped on his way, and when he drew rein at the gates of the station he felt equal to any unpleasant emergency. Not as the friend did he come now, but as the magistrate, an officer of the law; one in whom authority is placed, and who must prove himself worthy of so sacred a trust.

Mr. Franklin was in his daughter's room when the squatter rode up, but upon learning the name of his visitor he made all haste to join him in the study, whither that exalted being had adjourned.

"What's this about Miss Franklin?" asked the Member as soon as her father entered. "The servant said something about her being ill. What is it? Nothing dangerous, I hope."

"Indeed, I hope not. She is rather feverish and has been quite unconscious. But we have had the doctor over from Desolation, and he seems to think but lightly of it."

"Fever, eh? I wonder how she caught it?"

Mr. Franklin answered rather confusedly, and Wingrove smiled to himself—that is, inwardly. He wondered if a certain arrest, the particulars of which he knew so well, had anything to do with it.

"When did this come on, Franklin? Rather sudden, isn't it? When I saw her the other day I thought she looked the picture of health."

"She has complained of a headache for many days past, being afraid to go out for her exercise on account of these bushrangers. Yesterday, however, she would go out, and seems to have caught a cold."

"Poor thing! Give her my very kindest regards and tell her that she need fear the bushrangers no more. They are captured."

"Not both?"

"How do you know?"

"I—I do'nt know; I simply ask."

"No, they are not both captured, but the leader is.

We shall have the other one, too, before he is much older."

"Indeed! I hope so." Mr. Franklin seemed to fidget nervously under Wingrove's glance. "But who—who is this man—this leader you have taken?"

"Our old friend Stanford."

"Stanford—good God!"

"Yes, who would have believed it?"

Mr. Franklin did not answer. He remembered at that moment the suspicion which had once before flashed through his mind; he recalled the interview with his daughter when she fell senseless at his feet; again he heard her moaning cry of "Tom! Tom! Tom!" This then was the reason why Stanford had sworn him to secrecy. The truth went home to him with the force of a great blow. Stanford had robbed the bank for his daughter's sake!

"The news seems to have upset you," said the squatter meaningly.

"I wouldn't have believed it, by Jove!" There was the old careless ring in the Englishman's voice. It annoyed Wingrove.

"That's where we differ, Franklin. I had always my suspicions of that young man, and it was I who laid him by the heels."

"You! But may you not have made a mistake?"

"I think not. To all other men the Wooroota

bank robbery was a great mystery; to me it was the simplest of simple things."

"But how came you to solve that which puzzled the whole country?"

"Before I answer that question, you must understand, Franklin, that I am here as your friend; though my duty as a magistrate should blind me to all personal considerations."

"My dear Wingrove, you can't possibly think that I know anything of this? I assure you, upon my honour, that if I had known——"

"If you had known that Stanford had stolen that three thousand pounds from the Wooroota bank, you would never have accepted it."

Mr. Franklin shrank back as though he had received a violent blow, but instantly regaining his composure said coldly, "I do not understand this extraordinary language. I have accepted no money from Stanford."

"I am delighted to hear it, Franklin. Pardon me, old friend, but I was afraid you had. Now I may ventilate my suspicions about that money without reserve." There was a wicked light in the squatter's eye as he spoke, which Franklin, looking up, saw, then dropped his eyes again. That look seemed to go through him, numbing his senses.

"Is there any necessity for you to speak of it?" he asked.

"Well, you know," was the reply, "Stanford's trial is sure to disclose some awkward facts. I, for one, shall have to tell how I entertained my first suspicion of him, which is simple enough when you come to look at it in my way. I knew that he had been closeted with you the day after the robbery, and I also thought, you will pardon me, that no other man alive—except myself—would give you three thousand pounds. If I am wrong, which I trust is the case, all you will have to do is to go into the box and give the name of the man who lent you the money. Otherwise there is no knowing what they might not bring home to you. Accessory after the fact—accomplice, even. Who can say where blundering Justice will stop once she begins?"

"Look here, Wingrove, we've always been good friends, and I know you wouldn't wilfully do me a bad turn."

"I would not," said Mr. Wingrove impressively, though Franklin thought he saw a peculiar quiver round the man's mouth.

"Then why mention this money at all?"

"Do you know what you are asking me?"

"Yes. But is not friendship dearer than duty?"

"But my honour?" said Wingrove.

"Will shine brighter for the sacrifice. I do not fear the most searching inquiry of my actions, but the shame, the suspicion, would kill me."

o

A strange light shot from the squatter's eyes. Placing his hand on Franklin's shoulder he said, " I will do as you wish—for her sake."

"Thank you, thank you."

The Member for Billabong had played another trump card.

CHAPTER XIV.

THE CRY OF THE CURLEW.

MR. WINGROVE had no sooner quitted the precincts of the camp than the sergeant, bearing the prisoner's breakfast, which consisted of a couple of thick slices of bread and butter and a cup of tea, approached the spot where Stanford lay.

"Well, Tom," he said cheerily, "how goes it?"

"Pretty well, thank you, sergeant, though I should have preferred my privacy unbroken."

"Well, you know, I couldn't keep him out," replied the sergeant. "It would be as much as my billet's worth. But come, eat up. We must be off in a couple of minutes."

"Where do we go, sergeant?"

"Euraya to-day; Wooroota to-morrow. They'll try you there!"

"I see."

Stanford then fell to and ate heartily of his meagre fare. He had not forgotten the curlew's cry of last night. He might need his strength presently. Joe was free, and what was more, not the slightest suspicion had attached itself to him. With such a cool, dauntless fellow at large anything was possible. Tom,

o 2

knowing his devotion, was well aware that that great-
hearted fellow would risk his life, as he had risked
his liberty, for his sake.   He therefore permitted the
sergeant and trooper Tim to mount him as before,
though on this occasion they rode three abreast with
Stanford in the middle, his horse being made fast on
either side to those of the troopers.

The sun had not risen above an hour when the
little cavalcade set out towards the north, and as
Stanford inhaled the fragrant, the *free* morning breeze,
he unconsciously sighed aloud.   His captors exchanged
looks, but said nothing; why disturb the poor wretch's
gloomy thoughts ?   Higher and higher rose the sun,
turning from a blood-red to a dazzling yellow and
transforming the blushing east to a pale gold, till
even that died away and the day was truly come.
For over an hour they trotted on in silence till they
reached a little creek at which they stopped to water
the horses.   Here Tom begged the sergeant to fill
his pipe for him, which that good-natured officer
did, and likewise placed it between the prisoner's
lips.   Tom thanked him with a smile and then
relapsed once more into a moody silence.   He had
been wondering all this time what had become
of Joe.   From every clump of trees or patch of
scrub they passed he had expected to hear the
curlew cry, but so far the journey had proceeded
void of incident.

At noon they were only fifteen miles from Euraya, and the sergeant began to look forward to the completion of the journey with evident anxiety. Several times during the latter part of this journey he had called a sudden halt, without any ostensible reason, though once they all three seemed to hear the tramp of a horse in the bush. Stanford most certainly heard it, and he doubted not but that the two troopers heard it also, for they exchanged meaning glances and closed in. Yet this might mean nothing: a stray horse, a boundary rider; it might be either of these. Stanford wanted more than the mere tramp of hoofs, and presently he got it. As they began to mount a somewhat steep hill, the horses walking slowly, there came from the bush on his right hand side the cry of a curlew. Clear and distinct it floated in the air, then died away with a lingering echo. It was Joe, sure enough. Tom felt his heart beat wildly; a new light shot from his eyes. He looked to right and left with an eagerness that did not escape the sergeant.

"A queer cry that," said the trooper. Stanford did not answer, but continued to pull more vigorously at his pipe.

"Them curlews," answered Tim, "is strange animals. Blest if I don't think they're the banshees themselves at times. When I hear them o' nights I think of the Ould Country, and the divil run away with me if I don't believe the bastes have got something of the ould gintleman in them."

"Then what about the jackasses?" asked Stanford.

"Sure an' there's no doubt about them at all," was Tim's reply. "They are the infarnal one entirely."

Then the trio relapsed once more into silence, but the sergeant, who was a zealous officer, and one who never felt that he really had his man till he saw the prison doors close upon him, redoubled his assiduity. Stanford's every action was watched, every look followed with singular intensity; but Tom, who had now regained his composure, defied the wily officer to penetrate his thoughts.

The road now ran for about half a mile through a thick scrub, and as they entered upon it the sergeant glanced uneasily around, but for shame's sake breathed no word of his suspicions. All he said was, "Come, Tim, hurry up!" and put spurs to his horse. The trooper Tim obeyed the order, but Stanford, pressing well forward, somewhat retarded the progress of his own animal. They, however, forced him into a fairly rapid trot, and just as it appeared that they would clear the scrub without molestation, the cry of the curlew rang out some twenty yards ahead.

"Forward, forward!" shouted the sergeant, digging his spurs still deeper into his horse's sides; but Stanford, with a quick movement, flung himself forward

on his horse's neck.   The trooper turned to him with
an oath and a threatening gesture, but at that
moment the report of a rifle rang out and the sergeant felt a pricking in the fleshy part of his leg.
His horse bounded swiftly forward for a few yards,
then staggered from side to side and fell headlong to
the earth, hurling its rider from the saddle.

"Bail up!" cried a stentorian voice from among
the bushes.   "Throw your hands up!"

Now if the sergeant had only obeyed this order,
as any wise man taken at a disadvantage would have
done, all would have gone well; but both pride and
duty forbade any such ignoble surrender, and he
attempted, kneeling as he was, to draw his revolver.
Before he could do so, however, the rifle rang out
again and he dropped forward on his face in the
dust.

But in the meantime the trooper Tim had succeeded in extracting both his pistols from their
holsters, and, after firing a volley in the direction
from which he saw the smoke issue, he sprang from
his horse using that animal as a shield.   In a moment,
however, that dreadful rifle rang out again.   The man
in ambush was not one to let a sleeping dog lie.
The trooper's horse quivered as though receiving an
electric shock and then fell like a beast in the
shambles.   Tim, now seeing that the bush was his
only chance, sprang towards the scrub with what

agility he could command. But he who passes
his life in the saddle is rarely smart on his feet.
Ere he could reach that welcome cover, the rifle
shrieked once more and a bullet crashed through
his brain. Throwing up his arms, as though to
clutch the air for support, he straightened himself
for a moment and then fell backwards without a
moan.

Stanford now sat up and glanced about him with
a look of the most profound horror, and the next
moment Joe, with the smoking rifle still in his hand,
bounded into the road. His face was very pale, his
eyes wide open and excited-looking, but hiding
his agitation beneath a careless smile, he advanced
to Tom and immediately began to loosen his bonds.
Neither spoke during this operation, but when it was
finished Devine looked up into his companion's face, a
half-frightened, half-imploring look, and said, " There,
mate, you're free once more."

" Free, yes—but at what price ? My God, do you
know what you have done ? "

" I think so. I've thought it all out. We shall be
outlawed : a price set on our heads. Well, what then?
We have only to die once. I don't think I shall ever
trouble the hangman."

" I would rather have suffered any term, any
torture, than you should have done this thing."

" I was sorry enough to have to do it, mate, but

there was no other way. I assure you, I never meant it to end like this. If that fool of a sergeant had only put his hands up like a sensible man, I wouldn't have harmed a hair of his head. I didn't want to shoot them; I have everything to lose by such an action. But I meant to save you, mate, come what might, and I have."

"You could have saved me without shooting him." Stanford pointed to the still figure of the trooper Tim.

"I thought of letting him go," said Devine, "but when I saw the sergeant fall forward I felt that I had killed him, and knew what would follow. Then something whispered to me 'Shoot him, too. No one will know then who has committed the crime.' I fired at him and he fell."

"Don't you know that there can be no hiding such a crime as this?"

"I suppose not, mate. It is a bad business. I know all they'll say about it, and I'm sorry it's done. But it was my life or theirs, and yours on the top of it. I meant to get you out of this mess; I have thrown you into a deeper one."

Here the sergeant, who still lay upon his face in the dust, uttered a loud groan. Stanford sprang from his horse, rushed to him and bore him a few yards into the scrub, where he sat the poor fellow up and administered to him a little stimulant; but he only opened his eyes once and then closed them for ever. The trooper Tim was next examined, and found to be already dead. As we have said, the bullet had gone through his brain. They lifted him up between them, bore him into the scrub, and then began to hide their crime. First they dragged the two dead horses some distance in the bush, and then, tearing a couple of branches from the nearest tree, they artfully contrived to obliterate all traces of the fatal struggle; though Stanford knew that were he to bury the corpses a thousand feet below the road, the law would find it out. Still, they hid all the more palpable traces of the conflict, and then mounting their horses set out for Mount Desolation.

For a long time they galloped on in silence, Joe leading the way like the accomplished bushman that he was; but at length their horses began to blow, and he drew rein.

"They have a tidy journey yet," he said, "so we must give them a chance."

"Where do you think of going?"

"Back to the cave. It is our only hope."

"But do you think it safe enough now? Remember, this affair will bring the police in swarms. Such a thrill of horror will go through the country that they will leave no spot unsearched."

"Let them search. If they're clever enough to find us we'll give them a good reception. But they won't find us, mate, because they will not, cannot, dream of our whereabouts."

"But ought we not rather to make an effort to clear the country?"

"We'll talk of that by-and-by. To attempt such a thing now would be sheer foolhardiness. They'd catch us before we got a hundred miles, and string us up like a couple of —— "

"Murderers."

"Well, Tom, I'm downright sorry I did it, I can't tell you how sorry, but why wouldn't they bail up?"

"But to kill them, Joe. It's awful, awful."

"Listen to me, mate—if we are mates still?—that day you jumped into the Darling, full flood though it was and hissing like a cataract, and brought me out more dead than alive, set the seal on my love for you. I swore then that I would be a true mate to you whatever happened, and that I would pay you back the debt I owed you. Well, I've paid it back. We're quits."

"I know, I understand. I am sure you did not mean to shoot the men, but that does not alter the fact that you have. That act, mate, has driven us beyond the pale of society. We can never again be men, but must crawl and hide as beasts and vermin do. I don't want to upbraid you, Joe, because I understand the feelings which prompted you to act, but I would give my right hand to undo this business."

"I understand," said Devine in a low voice, "and I am sorry. You have something to live, to hope for. You see, I have nothing in the whole world but my friendship for you. I never liked anyone half as well as I do you, and there is nothing I wouldn't do for you, matey, there isn't, upon my soul. The feeling which prompted you to 'stick up' the Wooroota bank prompted me to save you at all costs. We shall be outlawed now—at least I shall be."

"What do you mean?"

"I mean that there is no reason why you should suffer for any fault of mine. You were ignorant of my intentions, and consequently innocent of all crime."

"No, no, mate," said Stanford hastily, "it is not like that at all. I may abhor this business, may wish that we had never been born, but you have done all that one man could do for another; we must stand or fall together."

"But there is no reason," urged Devine, "why you should suffer too. Go in—give yourself up—tell all. A surrender is always weighed in a man's favour. Then when you come out, if Miss Franklin loves you as she ought, she'll be waiting for you, and you can begin a new life."

"And you?"

"Oh, what does it matter what becomes of me? There is no one in the world to cry when I go under. I shall wander about till I'm bailed up. Then I'll fight, and if they don't kill me I'll kill myself. There's nothing much left for me."

Stanford pulled his horse close to that of his companion and took him by the hand. "We're in the same boat," he said, " we sink or swim together."

The tears sprang with a sudden rush into Joe's eyes, so suddenly that he turned away his face to hide them.

"You had better not," he cried in a choking voice, " anything is better than that. With me walks the hangman always. I'm as good as done for, but you may be happy yet."

"Where you go, I'll go; what you suffer, I'll suffer. I made a rogue of you for my own ends, and I'll stand by you to the last."

"Then there's my hand on it, mate. We'll lie low for a time and then make a bolt for it. Once in Melbourne——"

"Melbourne?"

"Ay, Melbourne. The bigger the city the better for us. Once there we'll ship away to America. You understand?"

"Yes, yes. Oh, that it might be!"

"Why shouldn't it? What's to prevent it? You'll see, mate, you'll see. But look, there is the old

mountain.   A twelve mile run, if an inch.   Let us
hurry up.   Don't spare your horse, Tom, you'll never
want it again.   Mount Desolation," he added, as he
drove his horse into a long, swinging stride, "they
ought to have called it Mount Hope."

Stanford sighed.   He remembered giving it that
name on a very different occasion.

CHAPTER XV.

BEYOND THE PALE.

Now it was not possible that such a crime as that narrated in the preceding chapter could long remain unknown, though it came to light much sooner than even its perpetrators could have imagined. Sergeant Jones was to telegraph to Mr. Wingrove immediately upon his safe arrival at Euraya, and the squatter had calculated the hour in which he should receive the message. Therefore his astonishment gave way to alarm when the time came and passed, and two more hours slipped by and yet the dispatch arrived not. That something unforeseen had happened he guessed intuitively, for the sergeant, he knew of old, was a disciplinarian before aught else, and that the first thing he would have done after seeing his charge secure, would have been to dispatch the message. He therefore ordered his horse and galloped over to the Mount Desolation post-office, and upon inquiring learnt that no message had been received for him that day. This news confirmed his already strong suspicions, and he immediately wired to the constable in charge at Euraya asking if the sergeant had turned up, and upon receiving a reply in the negative, wired back

again the particulars of that officer's journey, and also
the name and condition of his prisoner, with instructions to institute an immediate search. In the meantime he had dispatched along the road the troopers.
available in the local camp, and it so happened that
they came up with the Euraya police while those
officers were bearing the bodies of the two unfortunate
troopers back to the town.

If the news of the Wooroota bank robbery had
excited the public mind, the particulars of the double
murder convulsed it.   People went literally bushranger mad, and the name of Tom Stanford grew
notorious in an hour.   Frenzied letters were written
to the papers denouncing the police, Government,
and every other thing of authority.   They demanded
the commissioner's immediate retirement, and in such
unmistakable terms, too, that that excellent officer,
at whom we have heard Mr. Wingrove sneer, determined to resign forthwith. All officials resign; it
is a way they have. A new man, a man of undoubted experience, was appointed in his place. The
Government bestirred itself also; passed an Act
outlawing the men, and placed a reward of two
thousand pounds upon the head of each.   Thus
were Stanford and Devine driven from the pale
of society; a price upon their heads; their hands
against the world, the world against them.   Like
beasts they were to be destroyed. Any man might

shoot them down as such, and gain both gold and glory.

For a while Devine's identity remained shrouded in mystery, which threw the glamour of romance around him; but the discovery of a criminal's identity is merely a matter of time. Those who had been picturing him as some gentleman gone astray, were rudely shocked when they were informed that he was only an ordinary bushman. The police, however, would rather it had been otherwise. They expected trouble from this bushman, for they remembered that it was simply a knowledge of the country which had enabled the Kellys to set them so long at defiance.

Then began a feverish search for the outlaws. Large squads of men were drafted from all over the colony, and it was jokingly said that it would be dangerous to fire a shot in the district for fear of knocking over a trooper. As Stanford had foreseen, they simply swarmed the country. Wherever you went you saw a policeman, or heard the ring of his horse's hoofs. And yet with it all—and there could be no doubt of their endeavours to unearth the outlaws—no clue to those desperadoes had been found. It is true the newspaper correspondents sustained the public interest with the most absurd rumours; but these, after a time, fell flat. Even the public will not stand an eternal gulling. Then the black-trackers were brought from

P

Queensland; in fact, everything that ingenuity and experience could do were done to no purpose: the police were baffled at every step. If the earth had swallowed the men they could not have disappeared more completely. Then the cry went up that they had fled the country, and since no trace, no sign of them could be discovered, there was some reason for believing it. For, argued the people very naturally, if they had been hiding, the police, who had scoured the whole district, would surely have unearthed them. Therefore, one of two things was certain: the outlaws had either quitted the colony or the district. Of that most people felt assured. The police, too, confessed themselves at fault, but, learning from experience, were content to wait. If you will only wait long enough you will see the rat creep from his hole.

To hide from the police in a district which swarmed with them, appeared to the general public to be an utter impossibility. And yet it was not, for if we climb to the left of that great frowning mass which people call Mount Desolation, we shall advance, when we reach to within eight hundred feet of the top, to the edge of a precipice which completely bars further progress, though opposite to it, some twenty-five or twenty-seven feet away, is another ledge, not quite so precipitous and at a lower level. Between these two yawns an irregular chasm of jagged granite, so deep, black and irregular, that from either side you cannot see the bottom, though if you strain your ears and keep very quiet you will occasionally catch the sound of rippling water. It is from somewhere in this chasm that the river Warrigal takes its source, and looking down into its sombre depths one can imagine it a fitting haunt for the great monster.

The police had trodden the brow of this precipice a dozen times, had stood upon the ledge at the other side and laughed and joked with each other, while all the time the very men for whom they searched were not only within a stone-throw of them, but were actually listening to their talk. For beneath the great ledge upon which we are standing is a cave, led down to by a most precipitous and dangerous path, and one that very few men would care to travel even to avoid the police. It is quite twenty feet below the ledge on which we stand. Little lumps of rock jut out here and there allowing the feet to rest, the fingers to grip; but unless those fingers be like steel, and the heart equally as strong, the chasm of the Warrigal yawns for its victim. If we, however, will risk that dangerous path, cling like a spider to the granite wall, we shall presently round a ledge which opens out as we advance, disclosing a large aperture, the entrance of which looks up the valley. It is therefore impossible for anyone on either side of the chasm to distinguish this opening. One would have thought that such a place would have remained a secret to all but the birds. Yet if we advance still further into this aperture we shall see the two men whose welfare appears to be of vital interest to every soul in Australia—from Cape Yorke to Cape Otway, from Port Jackson to Perth.

The cave is some thirty feet in depth and from eight to twelve feet wide, being a good ten feet in height at the entrance but lowering rapidly as you advanced, so that after going a few yards you were forced to stoop to avoid injuring yourself. Here there are stretched several blankets showing that it is here the men sleep, while in one corner are piled a lot of empty tins and two or three small biscuit barrels. But it is not of such things as these that we are here to chronicle, but of those two men who are sitting smoking and moodily staring away up the valley. For six long bitter weeks have they been cooped up in this dreadful place, afraid to stir, to light a fire; almost afraid to speak. They have heard the tramp of the troopers above, have heard them laugh and talk; have watched the sun wheel round yonder corner of the mountain; have watched the moon sail on and on till the sides of their prison hid her; have started at the cry of the curlew and shuddered at the laugh of the jackass.

Stanford, during this tedious period, was in a

continual state of nervous excitement. He would
tramp up and down the narrow limits of the cave for
hours at a time, speaking no word, but looking the
picture of despair. His pipe rarely left his lips, and
well was it that Devine had laid in a good stock of
tobacco or he would have gone mad. We have all
seen the lion or the tiger walk his cage; even so was
Stanford, though he felt imprisonment more acutely
than those lordly beasts, being cursed with the power
of thought. His companion, on the contrary, seemed
very well pleased with his quarters, and confessed,
once or twice every day—just by way of impressing
Stanford with his luck—that it was a much better
place than any condemned cell in the country. Long
ago Devine, risking his life as boys will, had accidentally
discovered this cave, and before he left his native
district to push his fortunes on the New South Wales
side, he had paid many a visit to it till he grew quite
familiar with its dangers. When the country rang
with the doings of the Kellys he used to wonder if
they had some such place to hide in, though at that
time he never dreamt that he should want to use it
for such a purpose. After the Wooroota affair, previous to which he had well-stocked the cavern, he and
Stanford had hidden here for a week, though immediately Tom went forth, which was much against
his companion's wish, he was captured. After the
shooting of the two troopers they returned to this

spot and kept close till the excitement had somewhat
abated.   Then, it being about a month since the
commission of the crime, Stanford proposed that they
should make a move, a suggestion to which his companion would not listen.   He, however, insisted, and
declared that he only wished to gain some intelligence
of Miss Franklin and the squatter, and Devine, seeing
that he was determined, offered to go in his place, an
offer which Tom was prevailed upon to accept.   Joe
accordingly went and was away a day and a night,
but on the second night Stanford, sitting lonely and
miserable, heard the well-known cry of the curlew,
and a few minutes after the wanderer rejoined him.
He had many things to tell; the huge reward offered
for their apprehension: the many rumours circulated
concerning them; the numbers of police that scoured
the district, and that it was the general opinion that
they had left the country.   Of private news there was
little.   Mr. Wingrove was still most assiduous in his
search for the desperadoes, so that it will be seen he
had not returned to town for the opening of Parliament, and consequently his great attack on the
Government was never delivered.   Mr. Franklin was
still at Koorabyn, though he was seen by few, for his
daughter was ill and he was proving himself a most
devoted father.

This last piece of news struck a chill to Stanford's
heart.   Alice was ill.   How ill he did not know, but,

lover-like, pictured the worst, and upbraided himself in loud and bitter terms, for had he not indirectly smitten her down? Had Devine been a wise man, or could he have foreseen the consequences, he would have torn his tongue out ere he had uttered this unwelcome news. From that moment Stanford became like one demented. He would go, he would see her. Perhaps she was dying—dead! Trust him; he would take care of himself if it was only for her sake. He would see her, have only one word with her, and then he would return and lie low till such time as they should set out to clear the country. Joe argued, protested against what he felt sure would prove certain capture, and for many days prevailed. But at length Stanford could bear the uncertainty no longer.

"Capture or no capture," he said, as they sat smoking and staring moodily up the narrow space of light which was all their view of heaven, "I go to-night. My brain will turn if I stay in this dreadful place another day."

"But why won't I do instead?" pleaded Joe. "They are not likely to take me; and if they do, what does it matter?" he added carelessly. "I can do all you want, and do it better. I tell you, the traps are simply swarming the place, and they'd nab you like they did before. Come now, don't you think, mate, that I'd better make the journey? I will undertake to see Miss Franklin, if she is to be seen, to give her any message you may send. I'll——"

"No, Joe, I must go myself. I'm not such a poor bushman as you seem to imagine, and if I can't elude the police I deserve to be taken."

"Then let us go together. We've stuck to one another all through. Why should we part now?"

"No, no. Two might attract attention; one will not. If they take me I doubt that it will be alive; though I want to live, Joe, because of her."

"But perhaps now——" stammered Devine.

"That is just it, mate. There is a vast gulf between the outlaw and the honest man. I must have it from her own lips."

"You love her very dearly, Tom?"

"More than my life. I seem to have no existence when apart from her. With her is everything."

Devine looked at him with his great brown wondering eyes.

"I'd give something to love like that," he said.

"It might prove your curse, as it has mine. Yet I would do the same to-morrow, and the next day, and the next, and so on till there was no morrow. Listen to me, Joe, and I'll tell you all about it. You knew from the time I gave up going to the town of a Saturday night that I must have fallen in love with Miss Franklin—I think I told you as much. Anyway, you could see what was going on between us. I began to save money with an object; that object was our marriage. But she would not marry without her father's consent, and that he was constrained to withhold. I told you of Wingrove and the mortgage, and how she meant to marry him to save her father. She told me it all one night, a night I shall never forget. Then, mad as I was, I determined to save her at all costs, and, you remember, I broached the subject of 'sticking up' the Wooroota bank. I knew it was show week there, and that there would be plenty of money in the place. The three thousand pounds I took I brought to her father and prevailed upon him to accept, telling him that I had borrowed the money from some friends in Sydney. But Wingrove discovered that I had visited Koorabyn the day after the robbery; he put two and two together, and this is the result."

"And what object have you now in view?"

"I must reassure her and her father concerning that money, for I have no doubt that Wingrove is playing as deep a game as ever. He must know, or at least pretend to know, that the money Mr. Franklin paid him came from me; consequently he will have that unhappy man once more in his power."

Joe opened his big eyes very wide and gave a low whistle. "I see—and so get the young lady after all ?" Stanford bowed his head. "Well, mate," continued the big fellow in a low, earnest tone, "I'm yours, body and soul. I think I've shown you that. Wooroota bank, or anything you like. Give the word and I'll guarantee to settle Mr. Wingrove."

"No, no," shuddered Stanford, "not that, if you wish us to remain friends. We have done enough in that line, Joe."

"I don't see that you have done so much."

"I'll share the blame, anyway. You understand now one reason why I want to go ?"

"Ay, mate, I understand everything, and can only say good luck go with you. It's a pity you won't let me do for Wingrove, though."

"No, no; we must have no more of that. Yet if I ever meet him, Joe, as man to man, one of us shall take the long journey. We have everything to fear from that man. He hates me and will leave no stone unturned to hunt us down. They," he pointed towards Koorabyn as he spoke, "have even more to fear than we, for we can protect ourselves. He is the only one who knows their secret; if he were gone there would certainly be hope for them—there might even be for us."

"You will have every chance of meeting him," said Joe. "He prowls the country like a trooper, and has offered an extra thousand pounds to anyone who will take you dead or alive."

Stanford's lips went together and his eyes gleamed dangerously.

"Take me, eh ? You never told me this."

"I didn't like to."

"My dear Joe, you have a delicacy for which few people would give you credit. I shall be the more careful, and keep a watchful eye on Mr. Wingrove."

CHAPTER XVI.

HOW THE WOLF WENT FORTH.

THE rest of the afternoon was spent by Stanford in preparing for his departure. Though about to place his head in the lion's mouth, he yet contemplated the proceeding with marvellous equanimity, and hoped that noble animal would permit him to withdraw it again. He knew the principal danger would lie in his endeavours to obtain an interview with Alice, an incident which could only be brought about by stealth, and stealth in these times would quickly lay one open to suspicion. He had no doubt, either, but that Wingrove, who seemed to know human nature pretty well, would consider Alice's presence at Koorabyn a magnetic one, and would in consequence have the place well watched; but he trusted in his love and the dauntlessness of his own heart to lead him safely through the labyrinth. He would see her again, come what might; hear from her own lips his doom, and live or die as she might wish. He wondered what she would think of him. Was not his name a horror in the land, synonymous with murder, rapine—a thousand imaginary crimes? He was no longer the Stanford he knew, but a monster

whom the righteous could not regard with aught but
fear and loathing; a scourge, a pest—one whom it
would be an act of mercy to slay. Yet in his heart
there was none of that guile with which the world
credited him. Rather was he a wretch to be pitied.
But the fiat had gone forth. He was the lawful
prey of the community—hunted, banned; nought
but his death could atone for his iniquities. He
knew this was how they would think and speak of
him; he, God forgive him, had judged others almost
as harshly. How little he dreamt of the wretchedness that was theirs; how better than aught else
was that death for which the people clamoured so
loudly.

His disguise was not of a very elaborate nature,
for he already looked the bushman to perfection. His
beard had grown during his six weeks' incarceration
in the cave, but was too short and thick to answer
the purpose well. Over it, however, he fixed the long,
straggling beard which he had worn at Wooroota,
pulled Joe's old felt hat well down over his eyes, and
assuming a loose, slouching gait and a rough tone,
was declared by Mr. Devine to be passable. In a belt
beneath his shirt he carried a revolver and some
money, while over his shoulder he slung a coarse, blue
blanket done up in swag fashion.

"I think you'll do now," said Mr. Devine, eyeing
him critically. "You ought to pass muster if you

play your game properly. It is a dangerous game, Tom."

"All the more necessity for careful play."

"They nabbed you last time you saw her. Be careful, old man, be careful. It is a thousand to one she will be watched day and night; everything she says or does will be reported. It will be no easy thing to approach her, and I want you to avoid all risks. I've never said a word of this before," continued the big fellow in a voice that quivered with emotion, "and you won't mind me speaking of it now, because I'd do the same again for you, matey, but it would kill me if you were taken. Don't think I'm afraid to face what I've done, because I'm not, but if they were to take you I couldn't help asking myself why I became what I am."

Stanford seized his companion's hand and pressed it with a vice-like grip; but he said nothing. His heart was too full for words, besides, what could he say? This man had been honest all the days of his life till he had led him into evil ways. For his own ends he had made him first a thief, then a murderer, and now the shadow of the gallows fell on him everywhere. He had gained nothing by outrage, but the ever imminent, ignoble, and violent death. It was to further no interest of his, to put no money in his pocket, that he "stuck up" the Wooroota bank; it was not to save his own life that he shot down the

troopers. In every action he had shown the un-
selfishness of his devotion, the staunch, if reckless,
quality of his spirit; and though that spirit had been
displayed in an evil cause, it seemed to him a duty
to the mate he loved so well. Had he been one
whose lot was cast in higher places, he would never
have fallen into these emotional errors; but he had
lived all his life in the great " up country," had spent
his days amid the wild and the ungodly, and his ideas
of right and wrong must have been stunted in consequence. Stanford knew all this, and as he sat at
the entrance to the cave watching the sun's shadows
on the rocks and longing for the darkness to set in,
he felt such bitter pangs of remorse that he dared
not speak to his companion for fear of breaking
down.

At last the hour crept round; the sun had gone,
and the shadows began to envelop the mountains.
Away up the valley it was already dark, and beneath
the great rocks the gloom was deeper still. Then it
was that Stanford rose to his feet, and walking to the
entrance of the cavern scanned every available point,
and listened for a couple of minutes for sound of man
or beast. But he saw nothing, heard nothing. The
evening was as still as though the world were dead.
The great silent crags looked like the bodies of
petrified giants, and the yawning gulf at his feet
the path that led to eternity.

He stepped up to his companion, who sat puffing vigorously at his pipe, and took him by the hand.

"Good-bye, Joe."

"Good-bye, matey."

Joe turned his head aside as he spoke. There was something in his big brown eyes he did not want Stanford to see. Then the smoke got into his throat and nearly choked him, and amid his sputterings he was heard to curse his pipe in loud, ferocious tones. Tom turned aside, a strange lump rising in his own throat. Poor old Joe!

"You'll take care of yourself, matey?"

"Trust me. After this I will obey you in everything. I'll keep as quiet as you like till we make a move for England or America. Good-bye, old man."

"Good-bye, Tom."

Stanford seized his swag and slung it over his shoulder, and feeling that everything was in its proper place, began the journey. Joe accompanied him to the entrance of the cave, giving him a few directions as to the scaling of the ledge successfully, and how to behave so as to avoid suspicion once he reached the town.

"I shall expect you back inside the week."

"I shall be back then if I am alive—and free."

Joe marked the two added words, but said nothing. Perhaps it were better so. The next moment Stanford disappeared on his hazardous enterprise, while Joe, waiting till he heard the curlew cry, which was to tell him that Tom had reached the ledge in safety, turned back into the cave and sat smoking pipe after pipe till his brain reeled.

In the meantime Stanford had safely reached the ledge, and sitting for a moment to regain his breath, he seemed to realise that he was once more an inhabitant of the earth. The wide expanse of sky, with its already twinkling stars, seemed to him like the memory of some half-forgotten dream, and the pure air, as it sighed softly round his ears, seemed as fresh and free as hope. But he was not come to indulge his soul with the ideal. The task before him was one of a different nature. He arose with a weary sigh and continued his journey.

After traversing the rocky and uneven way for about a quarter of an hour, he rounded the base of the peak and stopped for a few moments to listen. No human sound, however, reached his ears, though away at his feet, lying in what appeared to be a great dark sea of air, he saw several twinkling lights, which proclaimed the whereabouts of the town of Mount Desolation. They were his goal, and towards them he set out, stopping every now and again to catch the sound of other footsteps, for one in his position thinks· even the very trees are dogging him. At length he reaches a more even way, and turning off to the left soon enters upon the regular mountain track.

Q

His progress is now comparatively easy, for the road is sure, and he can travel fast, without staying every minute to listen for the footfall of that invisible tracker.

At last his feet tread level ground, and presently he enters upon the high road which leads through the town one way and to Koorabyn the other. But the town is now his object, for here he hopes to pick up some information regarding the movements of the police. Slouching his hat well over his eyes, though the night is dark enough in all conscience, he swung along in true bush style, and the three people who bade him a cheery "Good-night" as they passed on their way from the township little knew the name and condition of the man whom they had thus accosted. That bush "good-night" is a grand old custom. How pleasant, friendly, hospitable, it sounds! Above you are the moon and stars, around you the eternal bush. Sometimes a night-bird screams, a frog croaks, and the great bats flit before the moon casting weird shadows on the road. An awe steals in upon you, and you feel so lonely that the very stillness of the night appals. Then away along the white road you see a shadow, and for a moment you wonder if it be a ghost or a man. It approaches, and the sound of footsteps rings out clearly in the night; it is a man. Presently you meet, you do not see his face, but as he passes you by he shouts out cheerily, "Good-night;" and you answer in the same tone, "Good-night to you," and you walk on feeling you could sing for joy—if you do not weep.

Pleasant indeed, like the memory of some sweet dream, sounded these greetings in Stanford's ears; and yet there was a ring of freedom in them, too, that jarred even while it pleased. There had been a time when he was always the first to shout those friendly words, but when spoken to-night they sounded almost like an accusation. He shrank within himself and mumbled "Good-night," and swung on as though he expected the man to turn, lay his hand upon his shoulder and say, "Tom Stanford, you are my prisoner!" Gone indeed seemed all that made life worth living. Poor is he who, having defied the law, lives in defiance of it. There shall be no rest by day, no peace by night. He will feel that eternal steel upon his wrists, and gaze upon the sun through imaginary bars. Poor Stanford! He was paying dearly for his crime. He felt that he would have given twenty years of his life to have been able to say "Good-night" as he had said it once. But he knew that would never be again. The world, which had once seemed so large, too large for even his imagination, had contracted to the four walls of a cell. There was now no room for him to breathe.

Past the police camp he stole, the very lock-up in which the unfortunate Sergeant Jones had chained

Q 2

him. He saw a mounted trooper issue from the gates and gallop off in the darkness. He slunk back in the shadows till the sound of the horse's hoofs had died away in the distance. Once he passed within a couple of yards of two members of that baleful organisation—passed so close to them that had they stretched out their hand they could have seized him; but it so happened that one was telling the other an amusing anecdote, and he was consequently overlooked. He, however, relished not such sudden meetings with that despicable class, but hurrying on to the other end of the town, entered a small hotel—they are all hotels—which was called the Wombat's Head—an indigenous name, so to speak. None of your imitative Boars' Heads, White Harts, Crowns and Sceptres, and such like foreign things, of which the young colonial knows next to nothing. Indeed, the dearth of native names to the public houses shows a lack of imagination truly deplorable, and is equalled only by dearth of native names to the towns.

Stanford knew the Wombat's Head by repute. It was a place frequented by fossickers, bullock drivers, and swagmen such as he was supposed to represent; and during the race week by the gentry who did the purse trick and manipulated the thimbles and the pea. Not that it was a low house, by any means. It was poor but honest, and the landlord

himself would tell you that there was not a better
regulated house in the district, and if you doubted his
word you might step out to the back yard with him
and he would prove it. But as the worthy host was
reckoned a bit of a bruiser few people accepted the
invitation. No; the worst people could say of the
Wombat's Head was that its patrons were poor
(except on race weeks), often unwashed, and oftener
still, like Jim Bludso, most careless in their talk. But
that they were all honest working men there could be
no doubt, for they would tell you so themselves;
indeed, they would simply pour their honesty and
hard work down your throat till it went close upon
choking you.

Tom hung for a moment or two before this para-
gon of publics, then walked boldly into the bar and
called for a pint of beer. This, upon being served to
him, he took over to a bench in one corner and sat
down. Then taking out his pipe he unconcernedly
began to fill it, though all the time he was narrowly
observing the other people in the room. There were
three of them, two being unmistakable bullock drivers,
for they spoke to each other in that caressing language with which they were wont to soothe the
labours of their teams. The other person might have
been anything from a shepherd downwards. Behind
the bar, in his shirt-sleeves, stood the landlord—a fat
young man with a coarse bloated face, no collar on,

and his dirty white shirt fastened at the neck with a
flash-looking diamond. On the fat little finger of his
fat right hand he had also an immense diamond ring
of the same quality. This jewel had evidently been
the cause of no little argument, and though they
stopped to look at Stanford when he entered, they recommenced as soon as they saw him go to his corner.
The two bullock drivers were wagering the landlord
thousands of pounds that the stone was not a genuine
one; not that they knew the real article from the
sham, but they had the popular vulgar notion that a
diamond was a jewel of inestimable value, and that
only princes and millionaires could afford one. The
landlord, however, attempted to convince them that
it was a brilliant of the first water, and offered very
graciously to prove the truth of his words if they
would step round to the back yard for about five
minutes—an invitation the teamsters laughingly declined.

"No, 'Arry, we're orf," said one of the men; "but
let us see if this swaggy knows anything about jools.
Hi, mate!" he cried, addressing Stanford, "do you
know anything about jool'ry?"

"I guess I know more about lumping my old bluey
here," replied Tom imitating the tone of the men and
patting his blanket as he spoke.

"Well, 'Arry 'ere says the jool is a reel diamond,
and I'm ready to bet 'im a thousand quid it ain't."

"Where'll you get 'old of a thousand quid?" asked the landlord contemptuously.

"Why at Wooroota, to be sure. Ain't they got a nice obliging bank clerk there, and don't they keep a lot of the ready always on 'and?"

Stanford started, and for a moment thought they were about to denounce him. Exiled from the busy haunts of men, he did not know how famous he had become, and that his so-called daring exploits were food for mirth and serious talk from one end of the country to the other. He kept his seat, however, and smoked the harder.

"There's lots of the ready everywhere, Jim," replied the landlord. "But we ain't all Tom Stanfords, you know."

"No," said the teamster as he wagged his head into his pot of beer, "we ain't. He's a remarkable fine feller is Tom, and I feel dashed sorry when I think of 'im being 'anded over to Jack Ketch."

"Well you know," began the landlord impressively, "the lor must be served. Not that I ain't sorry for him, you know, but what's to become of honest men if we don't trip up the rogues?" The bullock drivers here exchanged amused smiles, but out of deference to 'Arry's bruising capacity refrained from laughing outright. "You see," went on the worthy Boniface, "I feel for Tom more'n I can say, because me and 'im was like brothers. Many a good shillin' he's borrowed

of me, and he never passed by this shanty, Jim, but
what he dropped in to shake 'ands and say, 'How do,
'Arry.'"

Stanford listened in amazement to this tissue of
lies. He had never spoken a word to the man in his
life, and had never set foot in the Wombat's Head
before that night. He little knew that there were
hundreds of people in those parts who boasted of
intimacy with him simply to give themselves a little
importance. His greatness was quickly dawning upon
him, however, and he smoked on.

"He's a clever one," said the teamster. He had
made the same remark about a hundred times that
night. He was not a man of many ideas, but those
he had he stuck to.

"Clever," ejaculated the landlord, "clever ain't the
word. I'll tell you what it is, mate, we ain't 'ad such
a clever one as Tom since they 'ung Ned Kelly."

"But he *was* 'ung," said the shepherd. This
gentleman had not spoken before, but had seemed to
be entirely engrossed with his beer pot and his pipe.
However, his utterance was to the point, so much so
that it made Tom look up sharply at the speaker
He was a wiry-looking little man with a shocking
red beard and a pair of sharp grey eyes which, however, seemed to be closed half the time.

"Of course he was 'ung," said 'Arry the landlord,
"but wasn't it his own blessed fault? Was it the

cleverness of the pleece? No! And you mark my
word, old Carrots, when they take Tom Stanford
they'll know it."

"I ain't saying nothing against 'im," replied the
man with the red hair. "All I mean is that bushranging is a fool's game in these days." And having
delivered himself thus with marked emphasis, he
relapsed once more into the contemplation of his
pewter.

"I think you're right, mate," said Stanford, who
thought it incumbent upon him to say something;
"this chap you're talkin' of may be as clever as they
make 'em, but he ain't to be envied unless he's
quitted the country."

"And what if he has?" asked the bullock driver.

"But he ain't," said the man with the red hair.

"How do you know, mate?" asked Stanford.

The red-haired man looked a little confused. He
dipped his nose into his pewter before answering.
"Of course I don't know," he said.

"It's my opinion," said the landlord, "that 'im and
Joe Devine's gorne, and I shouldn't mind betting this
di'mond of mine that we never 'ear of them again."

"Perhaps you're in the know, 'Arry?" suggested
the red-haired man.

'Arry looked exceedingly important. He seemed
to expand till his fat neck bulged out over his shirt-
collar completely hiding the beautiful diamond stud.

"Perhaps I know a good lot, Sandy"—a vulgar
allusion to the little gentleman's hair—"and perhaps
I don't know nothing."

"'Arry's a knowing one," laughed the teamster.

"He is," said the shepherd.

"Here," cried Stanford rising, "fill up, 'Arry, will
you. Join me, mates?" he asked, turning to the
three gentlemen. The gentlemen required no pressing. They joined him with a will, and over the cup
that cheers while it inebriates Tom learnt much of
the notorious Thomas Stanford. That gentleman, it
seems, had been all over the country during the last
six weeks, playing at highwayman, burglar, and
general intimidator; though it was said that he
always treated ladies with the greatest respect (they
always do!) and that on one occasion he returned
a beautiful diamond locket to its lady owner because
it had inside a miniature of her dead child. (They
always have!) This was a very pretty story and
touched the bushranger's venomous heart, but when
he turned in for the night—the radiant 'Arry having
been able to accommodate him with the luxury of a
shake-down—he wondered much if he really were
that amiable though determined villain.

The next morning, after dispatching a hearty
breakfast, he set out on his tramp to Koorabyn,
passed unmolested through the town, by the police
camp and out into the bush. He looked away up

at the great mountain as he walked, traced the left side of the peak and pictured Joe sitting disconsolate before the entrance of the cave, the inevitable pipe between his lips. Poor old Joe! Dear, faithful old fellow! He breathed a blessing as he thought and then swung on. He passed several people on the road, but was surprised to see no troopers, considering he had been led to believe that the place was swarming with them. But about noon, as he approached a great partly-withered tree on which was stuck a placard headed "Murder," and which gave notice to the effect that the sum of two thousand pounds would be given for the body of Thomas Stanford, dead or alive, with a like sum for that of his associate, Joseph Devine—he beheld the red-haired man of the previous evening sitting at the foot of it pulling away complacently at a dirty little pipe.

"Ah, mate," cried the little man, "who'd have thought of seeing you out here?"

Stanford felt exceedingly annoyed at this chance meeting and would have liked to pass on with a shake of the head; but being afraid to do that which would have been easy enough under ordinary circumstances, he came and sat down beside the auburn one and began to smoke.

"So you're going Koorabyn way?" said the man. "That's lucky now, isn't it? I'm going that way too."

Stanford said he thought it was very lucky.

"They give a fellow a pretty good shake-down there," continued the man. "I know it, because it ain't the first time I've put in a night at Koorabyn. When Stanford was manager there——"

"Do you mean Stanford the bushranger?" How strange the question sounded as it left his lips!

"Of course I do," said the man with a laugh. "There ain't no other Stanford about these parts. But as I was saying, when he was manager he was pretty hard on us chaps, and wouldn't let a fellow put in a day to save his life. 'Loafin' about the place,' he used to call it."

"Well, he was quite right. He never refused anyone a night's shelter."

"How do you know, mate?"

"I suppose he didn't. Very few do."

"No; but don't you see," went on the little man with a curious smile, "his being a wrong 'un ought to have given him a natural sympathy with us chaps."

"Perhaps he was not always a wrong 'un."

"I suppose not, though it don't make no difference now."

"No."

"Look at that lovely bill up there," the man continued pointing at the placard above them. "'Murder!—Two thousand pounds reward!' Why mate, it's a fortin'. 'About five feet eleven inches high,'"—they were both standing now reading the

bill, "'long dark beard and large grey eyes.' Bless
me, mate," he added looking with a strange, quiz-
zing look into Stanford's face, "it hits you off to
a 't.'"

"It does sound a bit like me, to be sure; but, Lord
bless you, there's no counting on these descriptions.
What do you say, mate, shall we make a move?"
Tom did not like the little man's manner, and moreover, he saw now that he had made a mistake in
wearing the beard.

"That's him as he was at Wooroota," said the
man with a laugh; "this is him as he is. 'About
five feet nine inches high, broad shouldered, light
brown eyes and dark brown moustache.'"

"Well," laughed Tom, "they ought to easily find
him with two such descriptions."

The red-haired man chuckled oddly; said they
would be sure to find him in spite of a thousand
different descriptions, and then suggested that they
should make a start, though they were careful not
to approach the station before sundown lest they
might be sent further on. It is a custom in the
great up-country to give these tramps, swagmen, or
sundowners, as they are often called, a night's shelter
on the understanding that they shall be up and away
at sunrise, and so well do the men themselves understand this that they rarely have to be told to go,
though there are, of course, exceptions. It was in

this guise of tramp or sundowner that Stanford re-entered the well-known grounds and obtained, with his red-haired companion, the necessary lodging.

After a fairly substantial, if not epicurean repast, they were shown the hut, or out-house, in which it was permitted them to pass the night. There was no need of this little attention in Stanford's case, as he knew every inch of the ground, and had many a time come to this spot at sunrise to waken the tramps and send them on their way. But their guide was not supposed to know the quality of the lodgers. The hut, a low wooden building, was used for the storage of wool in the season, and for a thousand and one things out of it. It was, however, a safe and comfortable shelter, and Tom spread his blanket in one corner, the sandy-haired man in the other. While they lay smoking and talking an incident happened which forcibly brought home to Stanford his painful position. A trooper poked his head in at the door, and inquiring who was there in an authoritative manner was about to enter to examine the men, when the red-haired man arose in a towering passion, and striding over to him indignantly demanded by what right he molested honest men. The trooper surveyed the little man with amazement, laughed aloud at his vehemence, and then went off shutting the door behind him.

"Curse them troopers," said the man as he flung

himself down in his corner, " they give themselves more airs than a prince."

Tom said he thought they did, and declared that their powers should be curtailed, as an honest man was not safe with such a pack of rascals let loose upon the country. The red-haired man chuckled, said he believed him, and then relapsed into silence. But Stanford felt exceedingly uneasy, and wondered what he should have done had the trooper come and laid his hand upon his shoulder. And why had he not followed out his first intention? Why, also, had his companion bounded so suddenly to his feet and stormed so much about nothing? And why—this puzzled him most of all—why had the trooper allowed himself to be bullied in such an unreasonable manner, and, instead of retaliating, betaken himself off with a laugh? Tom grew uneasy as he thought of these things, and for the first time regarded his companion with suspicion. Then his suspicions took the shape of a horrible thought: he dressed the little red-haired man in a trooper's uniform, and, behold, he had the bogie by his side. Then he laughed at himself for being a suspicious fool, and knew that he had been dressing every tree in a similar manner. Madness takes various shapes and forms. Some dwell for ever in the Fortunate Isles; others see rats and various evil spirits. Stanford saw nothing but a trooper's uniform—a much more formidable apparition.

He watched his companion through the gloom, watched him with an eagerness which grew almost savage; any attempt on the part of that worthy to quit the hut would have been met with instant opposition. Luckily for both no such attempt was made. The man smoked on quietly for a considerable time, then knocked the ashes from his pipe, and with a "Good-night, mate," settled himself to sleep. Soon his loud, steady breathing told the watcher that he was in the land of dreams; and yet for fear that he was not, the watcher kept his vigil for two long hours. Then arising softly to his feet he groped his way to the door. He stood for a moment to listen.

The red-haired man slept on.

CHAPTER XVII.

WHY BOOMERANG WAS KEPT SADDLED.

WHEN Miss Franklin fell fainting at her father's feet, that worthy man little imagined the cause of this sudden catastrophe, though as he loosened the neck of her dress, and put a glass of water to her lips, he thought he heard her mutter the word "Tom." In a moment he guessed that something of importance had happened, and not having felt entirely secure, so to speak, regarding Stanford's loan, he nursed his daughter patiently till she came to, and then learnt of Tom's arrest. It may easily be understood how well he appreciated the situation, but putting a bold face on he told her everything would come right in the end. Leading her to her room he left her, but when he re-entered his study once more his face was like that of a corpse.

The girl slept not all through that dreadful night. Now and again she would doze, but it was always to dream such fearful things of Tom that she was glad to lie awake and stare into the darkness. When they came to her room in the morning they found her lying with a flushed hot face. She was in the first stages of a fever. All through that day she lay like one in a

R

dream, but that same night slept better, and the next morning was able to sit up and eat some breakfast. Then came the news of Stanford's escape and the murder of the troopers, and she knew that the last hope was gone. Two hours afterwards she was in a raging fever, and for three days she lay unconscious. She never spoke, save to utter the moan, "Tom! Tom!" All through that time her distracted father rarely left her side; and when she at last awoke to the world the first words she uttered were, "Is he taken?" Her father sighed deeply and told her that he was not. She smiled up into his face like a pleased child, and closing her eyes slept on for many hours.

From that moment she slowly but surely improved, and though it is now six weeks since Stanford's famous escape, she is not yet permitted to rise from her bed, though she sits up by the hour, and says she is as well as she will ever be. But the small settler's wife who acts as nurse is a fussy, kind old lady, and declares that Miss Alice will not be her own dear self for another month at least. At this the girl laughs, but always with such a tone of melancholy, that the good woman thinks her patient really worse than she is. Her father, however, understands that laugh, and when Mr. Wingrove, who sends her dainties every day, hears of it, he understands it also, and wonders if her heart is broken.

We have said that she was not permitted to arise

from her bed, and in this we are slightly incorrect, as
at noon every day she is led to the window of her bedroom to see her horse Boomerang, saddled and
bridled, led up and down before her eyes.   Three
weeks ago she conceived this idea, and every day
since then the sick girl's whim has been gratified.
Boomerang is kept day and night in harness, the
bit only not being between his teeth.   The people
about the place pitied the poor girl, for they thought
the fever had unhinged her mind; and even her
father had broached this subject to her.

"Do you not know what I mean by it?" she
asked.

"Indeed, I do not."

"Then let me tell you.   I will not believe that Tom
has left the country.   He will come to me first.   He
may want a horse at a moment's notice—a fleet horse,
one that will outpace the police.   Boomerang is ready."

And so the horse was carefully exercised every
day by one of the hands, and from the rider's own lips
she would have the daily report, "He's as fit as a
fiddle, Miss."   Then, and not till then, could she go
back to her weary bed.   Whether all this care and
foresight were to be wasted or not we shall presently
see.

Each day during her illness Mr. Wingrove had
either sent or called for news of her condition.
Indeed, he had shown himself of late in a most

agreeable light, for, looking upon Stanford as a dead man, he could afford to be magnanimous. He still held the secret of the bank-notes, knowing this would prove a more effective weapon than even the mortgage. It was unfortunate, truly, that the girl should have fallen ill about this time; and yet, perhaps, it was just as well when he came to think of it. Now she could possibly hold no communication with her lover, and by the time she was able to do so, they would have that lover's body, dead **or alive.** What had become of that person, Mr. Wingrove plagued his brains day and night to discover. That he had left the country he never believed for one moment, for such people rarely leave the spot they know. Moreover, in such a wild, half-civilised district he was sure to know plenty of people who not alone would give him information respecting the movements of the police, but who would also shield him from the vigilance of those officers. Yet Mr. Wingrove, though he confessed himself nonplussed, would entertain no thought of being beaten. It might be a waiting game, but the law would win, as it always did.

It had also been a custom of Alice's to have herself duly posted with a list of the latest arrivals at the station. This was done through the medium of her father, who entered into all her little secrets, but who never for one moment imagined that Stanford would be imprudent enough to venture near Koorabyn.

Indeed he believed, with a large section of the community, that the outlaws had long since quitted the country, but since it was his daughter's wish—and she had grown doubly dear to him of late—he had brought to him a list of all persons who came and went. These lists, it must be confessed, were not very entertaining reading, besides being singularly vague. His report for to-night ran: "Two sundowners—on their way to Wooroota"—nothing more. She closed her eyes with a sigh. It was the same story from week to week.

She turned to her book again and read till the words danced before her eyes. The nurse sat dozing in an armchair at the side of the bed; the night air stole in soft and cool through the open window, a big moth fluttered for a moment round the lamp and then fell into the devouring flame.

"Nurse!"

"Yes, Miss." The good soul shuffled to her feet and rubbed her eyes in a guilty manner.

The girl laughed. "Sit down, Mrs. Maxwell, pray do. I only wanted to ask you a question."

"A question?" queried the woman.

"Yes. Don't you think it would be the sweetest thing on earth to marry the man you loved?"

"Lord bless you, what have I to do with such thoughts as that?"

"But did you never have such thoughts?"

" I suppose so, Miss. They're foolish dreams that come to all women alike—especially when they're young."

"And do women no longer dream when their youth is fled ? "

" They dream of the past, my dear. If it has been a happy one, the memory of it will live for ever ; if it has been gloomy, the less thought you give it the better. Yes, I should say," she continued, as if speaking to herself, "though I am an old woman now, and try to forget such nonsense, that it would be the very sweetest thing on earth to marry the man you loved, providing that he also loved you."

" But supposing—supposing he was not worthy of a true woman's love ? "

" How do you mean, Miss ? "

" Supposing he did something wrong—something criminal ? "

" It all depends on the nature of the crime."

" Suppose he had sinned to shield you, and that in all other respects he was as honest as the day ? "

" I would take his hand in the face of the whole world."

A soft sigh escaped the girl's lips, and on looking up Mrs. Maxwell saw that her patient's face was buried deep in the pillow.

" What is the matter, dear ? " asked the old lady anxiously.

"Nothing, nothing!" cried the girl, looking up through tear-stained eyes. "I was only thinking how happy you must have been to marry the man of your heart."

The nurse shrugged her shoulders. "I have nothing to say against Maxwell," she said patronisingly. "He has been a good husband and father, and I have tried to do my duty by him, and, thank God, we've sailed our boat in pretty smooth water; but he wasn't the man of my heart, Miss, all the same."

"Tell me of that man," cried the girl, "oh, tell me of him!"

Ever since she had been a child she had known the staid Mrs. Maxwell, but had never imagined her the heroine of a romance. Indeed, the settler's wife was the last person that one would have connected with anything romantic; but if we stay to think of it we shall remember that even the lowest dream, and that there is a light in the eye and a smile on the lips for every man and woman.

"It was Jim," began the good woman, "Jim Andrews—as wild and handsome a boy as ever sat a horse. But he fell into bad company—went wrong, Miss—and they put him away for five years."

"But you waited, surely?"

"Yes—I would have waited a lifetime for him. But when he came out he wrote me a letter in which

he said that he would never drag me down to his
level; that a girl—I was a girl in those days, Miss—
that a girl like me must never mate with a felon. He
was going to the other end of the world, he said, but
he knew he should never see anyone who would take
my place. His letter was written from a public-house
in Melbourne. I replied immediately, telling him
how I had waited; that I cared not what he had
been; that I loved him then as I did in the old days,
and that I was willing to follow him through the
world. A week after my letter was returned. He
had left the place."

"And you have never seen nor heard of him
since?"

"Never."

"Poor thing!"

The girl threw herself back on the pillow with a
sigh; the nurse seized the opportunity to wipe the
unbidden tears from her eyes. So is it from the king
to the peasant, the palace to the hovel; and one is as
great as the other.

Alice lay thinking of this poor woman's dead
romance, and unconsciously intertwining her own story
with it. Both were sad, but oh, how much sadder
was her own! There would be no respite for her
lover, no chance of his living down his one act of
folly. Only with the sight of his body lying stiff in
death would the law of the land be satisfied. He too

might go to the other end of the world, but fate would dog him even there. Nor earth nor heaven would rest till he had given up his life. A murderer, an outlaw! a fugitive with a price upon his head— hunted, execrated, feared! She should forget, should hate him! A thousand times she told herself this harsh truth, and could she have believed he was the hideous monster the world would make him, she might have sunk her love in shame; but she *knew* he was not. They did not know him; how could they judge? But she knew why he sinned, and for whose sake, and she was woman enough to love him in the face of the world.

But suddenly her cheek turns deadly pale; instinctively she rises on her elbow. Through the window comes the low cry of a curlew. She can scarcely credit her senses, and falls back like one in a dream. But it is no dream, for in a few moments comes the weird cry again. A third time it is repeated, this time more plaintively—a low, heartbreaking appeal. Even the nurse starts from her dream.

"Dear me, that's a strange noise."

"What was that, Mrs. Maxwell?" Her voice quivers so that she can scarcely ask the question.

"I thought I heard a curlew crying; but it sounded so like a human voice that I'm not sure I wasn't dreaming."

"Dreaming, no doubt. You must be very tired, dear, so pray go to bed and have a good sleep. I shall want nothing through the night."

"Then I will go, Miss, for I assure you that I am quite drowsy. If you want me you will not forget to ring?"

"No, no; good-night. Tell my father, please, that I am better, ever so much better, and that I am very tired and sleepy." The good woman stooped down, kissed her tenderly, and then softly departed.

As soon as the door closed upon her, the girl darted from her bed and extinguished the lamp, a proceeding which, coupled with her intense excitement, almost laid her prostrate on the floor. With a great effort, however, she regained her bed, her heart beating so violently that it seemed as though it would burst. There she lay, however, her eyes glued to the open window, and presently the head and shoulders of a man appeared. For a moment or two the figure remained quite motionless. Then it whispered softly, "Alice!"

Her heart stopped beating so suddenly that she thought she would have died.

"Tom!" she gasped, "Tom!"

"Yes," replied the figure in the same low whisper, "it is I—Tom."

"What—what are you doing here? It is dangerous."

"I know it, but I have come to say good-bye. They told me you were ill, and so I had to come."

"Tom," she whispered, "come to me."

In a moment he had entered the room, and kneeling beside her bed covered her hands with kisses.

"They said you were ill, dear," he repeated, "and I, knowing the cause of that illness, have suffered the pangs of the accursed. But you say you are better now? Thank God for that, at least."

"Yes," she answered, "I am quite well and strong again and might get up if I pleased. But they tell me I shall get well sooner if I keep to my bed, and as they are all very good to me, I obey them. But you, Tom?"

"Well?" He dropped her hand as he spoke, a great sigh escaping him. She took his hand between her own.

"I know everything," she whispered in her sweet, low voice. "It was for my sake you sinned, and I would willingly share your punishment."

"Then you do not hate me?"

"Hate you! Oh, no."

"You do not think of me as the outlaw, the murderer?"

"I think of you only as the Tom I knew in the old happy days."

"Surely this is love?" he said half-musingly.

"Yes," she answered, "it is love."

"Alice," he said, "the man you love is not so unworthy of that love as you imagine, though he is unfit
to touch your hand. I am as innocent of bloodshed
as you yourself."

"Tom!"

"Hush, dear, or they may hear you. No doubt
the world is ignorant of the manner in which the two
troopers met their death, for who was left to tell it?
I know that I am outlawed, that a price is set on my
head, that I shall suffer ignominiously if ever I am
taken; and yet I am innocent of that dreadful crime."

"I knew it, I knew it," she sobbed. "Oh, I knew
it."

"You, at least, could trust me?"

"Always, always."

He then told her how he was taken to the Mount
Desolation lock-up, how he heard the curlew cry,
and how Joe had shot the troopers down.

"If you can prove this," she said, the narrative
having greatly excited her, "they will not—they will
not harm you." She could not speak the dreadful
word that came uppermost. The very thought of it
frightened her.

"I could only escape," he replied, "by turning in-
former. That, dear, is out of the question. But
there are other countries than this, Allie. There
is Europe—America—South Africa. In any of these
places there might still be a chance for a fellow to go

straight. But it is not altogether of myself I have come to speak," he added in a different tone, "for you, too, have a great danger to contend with."

" I ? " she said. " What is my danger ? "

" You do not quite understand, dear, you cannot ; but—but—let me speak plainly. If our arch-enemy——"

" The squatter ? "

" Yes, the squatter—if he chooses he may prove troublesome yet. The money I sto——I got at Wooroota went, as you know, to pay off the mort-gage ; that money may be, most probably is, still in the squatter's possession, and as he knows it is a part of the spoil he may hold it over your father as a threat. Have you heard anything of this ? "

" No ; I have been so ill ; though I have heard father say more than once that he would rather have died than touch a penny of it. But there," she added sadly, "it is a pity we did not all die before this trouble came upon us."

Stanford bowed his head.

" Still," he said, " it has come and we must bear it as best we can. What I wanted to tell you was this. If—if we should never meet again, and Wingrove should presume on his supposed power, you will defy him, mind you, for that money is absolutely un-traceable. I destroyed all books and papers that could in any way lead to its identification. Bear that

in mind always. Do not forget to tell your father
this. Wingrove may threaten, but he is powerless.
And now about ourselves, dearest. I will not attempt
to hide from you my danger. The police swarm the
country ready to shoot me down, and it is said that
even private people, tempted by the reward, are trying
to run me to earth. I am a monster let loose upon
society, a murderer, robber, outlaw. Every honest
hand is raised against me ; my death, no matter how
violent, will be greeted with acclamation. In fact, I
am one whose presence in this world is a degradation
to it, and whose death will be the only fitting penance
for a life so vile."

"Why do you say these dreadful things ?" she
sobbed.

"Because I want you to see me by the light of
the world ; because I want you to forget, if you can,
that you ever knew such a degraded wretch."

"Can I forget who was the cause of all this
misery ? Can I forget myself—the evil I awoke
in you ?"

"You must forget everything that will cause you
pain. And, after all, why should you take upon yourself the weight of my burden ? You did not urge me
to crime ; if you had done anything it would have
been to point the way to heaven. No, no ! it was
my own selfish nature that led me on. I would
have stopped at nothing to possess you."

"To save me.   Ah, don't belittle yourself like this, because I know, I feel;—and the world is harsh enough for us both now.   I am only a poor, sickly girl, Tom, but while I breathe I shall love you in spite of all."

Stanford pressed his lips to hers murmuring passionately, "Oh, God!   My God!"

"Don't give way like this," she said in a choking voice, "the time has come for action.   You have been here too long already—you should have fled the country weeks ago.   By this time you would have been safe on the seas, and in some foreign country the facilities for a newer and better life might have been given you."

"I could not go without seeing you; without knowing what you would say."

"I was afraid of this; but now you have seen me you must hesitate no longer.   For the last three weeks I have expected you, and I have had Boomerang kept in a state of readiness.   Take him, he is yours.   Go—and heaven bless you."

Stanford kissed the tears from her sunken eyes.

"Ah," he murmured, "if I were only worthy of you."

"Yes, you must go," she continued.   "While you are in this dreadful place I shall live a life of constant terror.   Once you reach some foreign country write to me and I will come to you."

"You will come to me?" he said in a voice full of wonder and love.

"To the end of the world."

How long Stanford knelt pressing those dear wasted hands he never knew. To him it seemed but a few moments; yet when he turned to the window the first pale shadow of day was already apparent in the east. With a start he arose to his feet. The girl lay sleeping soundly, a smile upon her face, her flushed lips parting on the pearls beneath. For a moment he hung over her with a hopeless, a despairing look; then turning softly away quitted the apartment.

CHAPTER XVIII.

THE CHASE.

By the time Stanford reached the hut the east began to lighten rapidly, so that had he prolonged his departure he might have been espied emerging from the precincts of the house—an incident which most probably would have led to his immediate downfall. As it was, he was lucky enough to reach the aforementioned hut without observation, though he thought he saw the door close suddenly as he advanced out of the semi-gloom. Upon entering the modest habitation, however, he was relieved to find his red-haired companion snoring away as complacently as ever. Indeed, that worthy seemed not even to have shifted his position all through the night.

Tom flung himself down in his corner and awaited the advent of day, for then both he and his companion would have to be up and moving. He would go back to the mountain and arrange with Joe for their departure. The tree of life bore yet the immortal blossoms of hope. He would quit the country, and in some new world strike out a new life. She should never regret her devotion; of that he swore a thousand solemn oaths. The past might be clouded,

s

but they would forget it, and the future should be the sweeter for the old dead sorrow.

At last the sun broke forth, a dull-red angry ball, and day came in with the rush of a whirlwind. Stanford rolled from side to side on his downy couch, yawned loudly, and then sat up rubbing his eyes, as though he had just awakened from a heavy sleep. Indeed, he almost wondered if his experience of the last few hours had been other than a sweet sad dream. His companion, however, seemed also to awake at the self-same moment; he sat up, rubbed his eyes violently, as though he intended to relieve them of their lids, and yawned till his mouth resembled a gaping chasm.

"Mornin', mate," he growled.

"Mornin'," said Stanford gruffly.

"What's the move this mornin'?"

"I have not yet decided."

"Oh well, it don't matter much. I ain't particular myself; so if you don't mind we'll tramp it together."

"Thank you," said Tom coldly. "I prefer to go alone."

"You *prefer*, mate, eh? Well, it's a free country, and a man may go whichever way he pleases. Good luck to you, mate; that's all I've got to say. Why, lor bless me," cried the man as he arose to his feet, "what have you done with your beard?"

Stanford started at this question, hastily passed his hand across his face, and discovered, to his horror, that he had lost his false beard.

"Oh," he replied with a smile, "I've been to the barber's."

The red-haired man laughed loudly; the joke was so excruciatingly funny. Yet had Stanford been less agitated he could scarcely have failed to perceive the excited nature of that laugh. He, however, busied himself with his swag, apparently oblivious of the man's presence and of the fact that he had asked an exceedingly awkward question. At length he swung the blue blanket upon his shoulder and strode towards the door.

"Good-bye, mate."

"Good-bye," said the sandy-haired man.

Tom opened the door and stepped out, turning his face towards Mount Desolation. The red-haired man watched him through the partly-opened door; his little eyes fairly glittered with excitement, his cheeks grew pale as death. "Will they never come?" he muttered; "will they never come?"

In the meantime Tom pursued his way towards the high-road, and as he approached the slip-rails which opened on to it he espied the figure of a man approaching him. The man he knew in a moment, and wondered if he himself would be recognised. There was little doubt of that, for as Mr. Franklin

s 2

approached (for he it was) he held his finger to his lips by way of warning.

"Tom," he said as he drew near to Stanford, "I gave you credit for more sense than this."

"Am I so easily recognisable?"

"At present you are. You should have taken more care of this." As he spoke he extracted the false beard from his pocket.

"Where did you get that, sir?"

"Where you should never have left it, Stanford."

"On my soul, sir—had your daughter been my own sister——"

"I know, I know. She sent for me—told me all. But that does not make your conduct the less reprehensible. Suppose it should be known that you——"

"Yes, yes, I was wrong. I hope you will pardon me. Your daughter shall never see me again in Australia."

"Then, you foolish fellow, there is your own safety as well. I have every reason to believe that you are watched even now. Tell me, did not a man with sharp ferrety eyes and red hair come with you?"

"Yes."

"Then keep your eye on him. If he's not a trooper, he's on the look-out for the two thousand pounds."

Stanford grasped the situation in a moment.

"I believe you're right," he said. "Nay, I'll swear he's a spy. He has watched me very narrowly at times, and—oh what a fool I've been!" he suddenly cried. "I can see everything now. No doubt he has given the alarm already?"

"Most probably. We had a trooper here last night; this morning he is gone."

"He came to the hut," said Stanford hurriedly. "He would have searched us had not the sandy-haired man abused him so."

"Then it's true enough," said Mr. Franklin, "and the best thing you can do is to sheer off."

"But surely they would have arrested me if they had been suspicious?"

"Who knows? You have a terrible reputation. Besides, the trooper may have had no suspicion. Someone else may have taken a message. Anyway, you are in danger; so you had better go. I don't ask where your hiding-place is; but wherever it may be, get there as soon as you can. It's ten to one that we shall have Wingrove and the police here before we have time to turn round. Alice has kept Boomerang ready saddled against a day like this. Take him and be off."

"But will the groom let me?"

"Say to him 'Boomerang's mine.' He will then help you in every way. Now I must go. Take care of yourself, Stanford—for her sake."

"Tell her, sir," cried Tom, "that I am hers, body and soul, in life or death." Mr. Franklin waved a good-bye, and Tom retraced his steps to the stables. And all the time the red-haired man stood behind the door of the hut absolutely quivering with excitement, and muttering between his teeth, "Will they never come?—will they never come?"

Stanford entered the stable without opposition, and found Boomerang already saddled and bridled. To tighten the girth, slip the bit between his teeth, and unfasten that splendid animal was the work of a moment. But he was not destined to pass out unmolested. At that moment the stable-hand (a new man, who had exercised the horse for the last three weeks) descended from the loft, where he had been sleeping, and, springing forward, seized the horse's bridle.

"Here, mister," he cried, "what are you doing with that horse?"

"Boomerang's mine," said Stanford.

"Right you are, mister." The man drew respectfully back as he spoke. "I've been waiting for you a long time. Who are you, eh?"

"Can you keep a secret?"

"I think so."

Stanford whispered two words in his ear.

"What!" cried the man. "By George!"

"Is there anyone outside?"

The man stole to the door and looked out.

"Not a soul."

"Then we'll make a move."

Tom led the noble-looking horse out of the stable, and was gathering the reins preparatory to mounting, when the little red-haired man bounded round one of the corners of the building, a revolver in his hand.

"Surrender!" he screamed at the top of his voice. "Bail up! You are my prisoner!"

Stanford was taken completely unawares; but, luckily for him, the horse was between him and the revolver, and as the man ran round to either apprehend, or get a better shot at his person, he was tripped up by the stableman, who was lounging in the doorway. The little man went sprawling to the earth, his revolver exploding as he fell.

"Here," cried the stableman, "what do you mean by rushing about like that with revolvers in your hand? You'll be shooting somebody presently, that'll be the end of it." And before the red-haired man could move, the stableman had secured the weapon.

Tom caught the man's eye; there was a merry twinkle in it, a smile played round the corners of his mouth. He nodded "Away!" Stanford was in the saddle in a moment, and the horse shot off like an arrow.

In the meantime the red-haired man arose to his

feet, quivering with anger. Shaking his fist at the stableman, he shouted, "I'm a trooper, I am, and I'll make you smart for this. That man is Tom Stanford!"

"Tom Stanford!" ejaculated the fellow, affecting a look of blank amazement.

"Yes, Tom Stanford."

"Then why didn't you say so? How was I to know who he was?"

"Two thousand pounds if a penny, and it's slipped through my fingers like water. Get me a horse, you fool—quick, quick, in the name of the law!" In a moment one was led forth; it had only a bridle on; but the trooper, disdaining such luxuries as a saddle, bounded on to its back with cat-like agility, and started off in hot pursuit. He had noted with joy that Stanford had taken the Mount Desolation road, and it was ten to one that they would meet the troopers, for whom he had sent, long before they reached the junction of the two roads.

Once Stanford had cleared the domain of Koorabyn he eased his horse, for he considered that he had now left all pursuit behind, and congratulated himself upon thus cheaply getting out of a serious scrape. But presently he heard the beat of hoofs in his rear, and upon turning round easily recognised his late travelling companion. So the affair was not ended yet. For a moment he remained irresolute. To run

away from one man seemed to him an unchivalrous
proceeding, and yet to stay would surely be to kill
him or get killed—one act being almost as bad as the
other. He therefore determined to run; and giving
Boomerang the rein, away the great horse flew. The
red-haired man discharged his revolver after him,
more by way of an earnest of his intentions than
any hope he might entertain of hitting his object.
Stanford smiled grimly. Give him no enemy in
front, and he could leave the trooper whenever he
pleased.

For about five miles the two horsemen held their
respective positions, Boomerang sailing along with
giant strides as easily as a bird. Not so the trooper's
horse. It had already shot its bolt, and was in great
distress. This in itself was bad enough, and almost
drove the trooper mad; while, to make matters worse,
the junction was but a little way ahead, and there was
no sign of that help for which he had sent. This
junction was where the Billabong road joined the
Mount Desolation road, and along the first-named the
troopers would come from Wingrove Station. "If the
bushranger," so ran the trooper's thoughts, "would
only turn up the Billabong road, he would run fair into
the trap;" but that was a piece of good fortune for
which he scarcely dared to hope. As they neared
the finger-post he saw, to his dismay, that Stanford
had no intention of thus obliging him, and his rage

grew so extreme that he discharged his pistol in the
air—for his aim at Stanford at such a distance could
be described as nothing else. Tom smiled and eased
his horse, knowing this was a dying kick; but the one
quick glance he took of the Billabong road as he
shot by the finger-post changed that smile into a
frown. There, not more than three hundred yards
from him, coming at full gallop, were six or seven
troopers, with—quick though the glance was, he could
see that—Mr. Wingrove at their head. No doubt
the recognition was mutual. Wingrove would have
known Boomerang, if not his rider.

Tom pressed the sides of the good horse and away
it flew. "For her sake, Boomerang," he cried—"for
her sake, old boy;" and as though it knew the meaning of those words, the grand horse flattened its
ears and swept on like an arrow. Before him, nine
or ten miles away, Stanford saw the great mountain,
now looming up clearly and distinctly in the morning
air. It looked no distance, not five miles; and yet
he knew it must be twice that sum. Should he ever
reach it, he wondered. He looked at the road beneath him. The horse seemed to skim over it like
a bird. He looked behind at his pursuers; they still
maintained their positions, Wingrove's great black
horse being still in the van. But Boomerang showed
no signs of fatigue. He might yet wear them down,
one by one—till he was left alone with the rider of

that black horse. They had a debt to settle, a long-standing grievance. There might be hope for one without the other, but for both the world was not large enough.

But presently Stanford was recalled to himself, so to speak, by the crack of a rifle. So they were trying pot-shots at him; and though he feared but little the correctness of their aim under such conditions, he yet knew that by some fluke either he or his horse might be hit at any moment. As it was, one bullet came close enough for him to hear its whistle, and another scattered the dust some twenty yards ahead of him. His hold on the rein tightened, and the great horse flew on like another Pegasus.

And so mile after mile was passed, till at length Stanford branched off from the road which led to the township, and made a dart for the mountain. The road was now much rougher, and he had to clear boulders, fallen trees, and no end of cumbersome obstacles; but Boomerang, though flaked with foam and wet with sweat, still swept on in his grand, tireless way. The last half-mile had been a terrible one; but the gallant animal had bested half of his pursuers, and the remainder were so battered and blown that they, too, soon came to a standstill—all but the big black horse. He still kept his feet, though cut and mangled with spur, wood, and stones.

When Wingrove saw his companions beaten, he
pulled up his horse and shouted to the men,
"Pick him off, some of you—for God's sake, pick
him off!"

The men fell upon their knees and fired; and as
Boomerang was at that moment skirting some huge
boulders about two hundred yards away, with his
whole side exposed to the fire of the enemy, he
received one of the bullets. He sprang forward for
a couple of dozen yards with renewed activity, then
staggered and fell to the earth.

A shout of triumph arose from the troopers, and
being at this moment joined by the other members of
the force, who had come up on foot, the party dashed
up the side of the mountain after the fugitive. It
seemed to them that Stanford's capture was now
reduced to a certainty; but that he intended to
surrender without a struggle they never for one
moment imagined. Every now and again some
trooper would up with his rifle and fire at the
bounding figure above them; but it continued to
rush on, as though it bore a charmed life. Wingrove
watched him with every nerve strained to its utmost
tension, and when he saw Stanford take the path
that led to the cave he gave a shout of joy. "Easy,
men," he cried; "we've got him now. Unless he
jumps into the great ravine he's ours, and even then
we'll get him. Two thousand pounds between six

of you. Not a bad day's work, my lads—not a bad day's work." He could have shouted for joy. There was no escape for his enemy now. They would take him, alive or dead. Alive, he would prefer, for the degradation which would ensue would be sweeter to him than honey. Yet take him they must, even though they riddled his body with bullets.

In the meantime Stanford bounded on, maddened by the cries of his adversaries, and wishing he had taken any road but this, for with such a horse as Boomerang he could have outstripped them all in the open country. Now he was leading them straight into the possession of the secret, and was thereby endangering Joe's life as well. Sometimes he thought he would stand and face about. He would fall, most probably, but he would save Joe. Then like a flash his thoughts would wander to the sick girl lying away out yonder, and repeating to himself her dear words, " To the end of the world," he would gain a new longing to live, to live! He bounded on afresh. If he could only reach the cave unobserved, he knew they would search for his body at the bottom of the ravine, thinking he had fallen into the chasm. There could be no other theory for such a mysterious disappearance. Then, then the time might come; the happy, happy future! Yes, life was indeed worth fighting for.

Up the rocky way he scrambled, onward, forward!

Now the bullets flattened themselves on the rocks around him, now they whistled by his ears with an ominous sound. Yet he seemed to bear a charmed life. He could almost laugh at their shooting, he felt the danger so little. Another fifty yards and he would reach some huge boulders, behind which he would find a temporary shelter. Under cover of these he might—yes, he might gain the cave, for it was not far distant now. The thought stimulated him to fresh exertion, and though tired and bleeding, he concentrated all his powers in a final effort. The run to the rocks aforementioned was somewhat open, but he thought little of this as he bounded on. Crack, crack, went the rifles merrily. It is fine sport to shoot at men! Tom had already crossed half the space when he felt a tingling sensation in his shoulder. Instinctively his hand went up to the burning part. It was met with a warm fluid. He had been hit. He stopped dead where he was, exposed to their fire, and drawing his revolver returned the compliment. The advancing troopers stayed their rush and looked about for some cover. At the same moment, and while both pursuers and pursued seemed undecided what to do, a rifle rang out, and one of the troopers fell to rise no more. A second shot quickly followed the first, and another man fell badly wounded.

"Down, men," cried Wingrove, the men obeying with alacrity.

From the rocks above came the cry of a curlew—a fierce exultant shriek. Stanford looked up and beheld Devine beckoning to him.

"Tom, Tom!"

The big fellow was gesticulating wildly, and even at that distance Stanford could see the excited look in his mate's big eyes.

"For God's sake, come!"

Tom seemed to forget the pain in his shoulder, the proximity of the troopers with their deadly rifles. There seemed to be a sort of security in Devine's presence; a protection from assault, from ill. With him all danger lessened. There was hope in the big fellow's eyes; confidence and determination in his movements. He was one to whom the weak would instinctively cling, the brave look for aid and counsel. Mild in peace, but terrible in war. One whom the good might love, the evil hate and fear. A child's heart in a giant's body.

In a few moments Stanford was by his side. No word of greeting passed between them, but Tom saw the look of reproach in his companion's eyes.

"Here," said Joe, pressing a rifle into his hand, "shoot!"

Stanford took the weapon, but could not raise it to his shoulder on account of the wound. Joe saw the pain in his face. The reproach fled from his look; his great eyes grew soft as a woman's.

"They've hit you, Tom?"

"Yes, slightly."

Devine ground his teeth and uttered a mighty oath.

"Curse them, curse them!   But we can fight yet, eh, matey?"

Stanford nodded.   He knew it would be a battle to the death.

CHAPTER XIX.

STANFORD'S LEAP.

THE troopers had in the meantime sought cover, and from behind the rocks began a desultory sort of fire, producing more noise than injury. Whenever the outlaws showed themselves, a whizzing bullet close by showed the watchfulness of the police; and on one occasion when Devine held his hat a few inches above the rock behind which he was sheltered, a ball passed clean through it. The big fellow laughed grimly, but replied to their attentions with interest, forcing them well behind their cover.

The outlaws certainly commanded the best position, for to reach them the police had to advance straight in the face of their fire; but they were weak in numbers, and the opportunities of shelter were so many that an advance, if actively carried out in skirmishing order, was sure of success. This Wingrove quickly saw, and ordered the advance accordingly, himself crawling from shelter to shelter while the constables covered his movements with their rifles. The sergeant in command of the detachment then followed the squatter's lead, being protected in a similar manner; the next and the next followed suit, until

T

the whole force had advanced in safety some dozen yards or more.

This manœuvre astonished as well as nonplussed the pursued. Stanford looked exceedingly grave, Devine as furious as an entrapped lion. His face grew hard as the rocks about him, and he clutched his rifle till the blood almost burst through his finger-tips.

"This is getting serious, Joe."

"It is serious, but we have no one but ourselves to blame. A good general should never fight on the wrong side of a stream, unless he's sure of winning. The ravine cuts off our retreat."

"It's my fault. I should have kept to the road."

"It would have been better, Tom, but it's no good talking now."

"We can fight, Joe."

"Yes, yes. There, look out!" He hurriedly discharged his rifle as he spoke, and received a volley in return. "Bah!" he laughed, "you can't hit a haystack. Yes, we can fight," he went on, "but the fighting's got to end some time, and, by appearances, it will be pretty quick too. Now it don't matter much what becomes of me, Tom. There's nobody in the world I care for but you, and, between ourselves, I am sick and tired of this sort of life. It's well enough for a dingo, but it's death to a man. Ha, there's another of 'em." Again he let fly with his rifle, and again a shower of bullets flattened themselves on the rocks around him. "You see, Tom," he went on, speaking quickly, but watching all the time with cat-like eagerness, "as things stand at present we're sure to go under, and I can't see why both should go."

"What do you mean?"

"This, Tom; that I'll hold the way against them while you get to the cave."

"No, no!"

"Why not? You may find security there. Lie low until this affair blows over, and then quit the country."

"No; don't speak of it."

"Remember," continued Devine in the same low, hurried voice, still watching every movement of his adversaries, "that there is another. For her sake, mate. She loves you still?"

"Yes, yes."

"Brave girl. Go, Tom, go—you have something to live for. Give me your hand, mate. Go, for the love of God!"

"Is there no other way?"

"None. If we were across the ravine, we might escape. It would take the troopers five or six hours to get round to the other side. But that can't be done, mate, can it?"

Stanford sighed. "Well, Joe," he said, gripping his companion's great brown hand, "I neither can nor will leave you; so set your mind at rest on that point.

T 2

We have gone so far together; we shall make the
great journey, too, if the worst comes, though I shall
regret leaving one man behind."

"Wingrove ?"

"Yes. If he were gone, she would have no enemy."

"I shall keep a shot for him, never fear. But look
out! they're up to something."

This admonition was given so suddenly that Stanford fully expected a rush, and was not altogether
disappointed, for the troopers, emboldened by the
quietness which reigned in the outlaws' position,
began to advance; and one in particular, impelled by
rashness or a burning desire for distinction, rushed
on ahead of his companions as though he would
storm the place single-handed. Devine marked this
man, and muttering between his teeth the word "fool,"
fired, and brought him head foremost to the ground.
With a grim smile he watched him roll over and over
among the rocks, and without changing his position
proceeded to open fire on the rest of the troopers.

Stanford saw the peril of his situation and shouted
to him, "Cover! For heaven's sake, don't expose
yourself like that!"

"Oh," was the answer, "they couldn't hit a hay——"
He clutched the rock against which he was standing
and sank to his knees. The word died in blood upon
his lips. A ball had torn its way through his throat.
His face was already ghastly pale: he breathed

whole volumes of blood. Stanford was by his side in a moment, and had the big fellow's head in his arms.

"Joe, Joe!"

The dying man turned his eyes up to his companion's face—a world of love in their fast glazing depths. He tried to speak; his chest heaved with the exertion, and with a sound that resembled a word the blood gushed forth. This, however, seemed to clear the passage.

"Done for," he gasped. "Good-bye, matey. Jump, jump!" He seized Tom's hand and pressed it to his bloodstained lips; then closed his eyes and fell back in a deathly swoon. Indeed, Stanford thought he was dead, and for the moment was paralysed with grief. But the cry of the advancing troopers quickly recalled him to the grim reality of his surroundings. They had seen Devine fall, and after waiting a minute to make sure, the word was given to charge. The men advanced in skirmishing order, Wingrove in the centre, crying at the top of his voice, "Surrender, Stanford—surrender!"

Stanford turned on him, utterly oblivious of the advancing troopers, took deliberate aim and pulled the trigger. But, to his mortification, the pistol missed fire. Again and again he snapped it, but without avail.

The man laughed aloud, though his red face had turned suddenly white and ghastly. "Don't shoot,

men," he cried; "we've caged the bird at last. Surrender, Stanford, or you're a dead man."

"Never," was the reply; and hurling the pistol at
his adversary he turned, his lips pressed close together, and ran towards the ravine. A sudden
thought had entered his head. He would jump, as
poor Joe had proposed. Often he and his companion,
while they lay cooped in the cave, had gauged the
width of that chasm, and they had concluded that it
might be anything from twenty-four to twenty-eight
feet. Even at the lowest computation he doubted if
he could leap so great a distance, though as a boy he
had been an active runner and jumper. He also
recollected that the opposite ledge was some two or
three feet lower than the one from which he would
spring. This, of course, would give him an advantage.
Onward he rushed, these thoughts flashing through
his mind. Before him lay fearful uncertainty, behind
him a certainty more fearful.

Wingrove laughed aloud as he saw the trap into
which Stanford was running, for he never for a
moment dreamt that he would be rash enough to
attempt such a leap, and the thought of suicide never
once entered his head.

"Don't shoot, men," he cried—"don't shoot."

The troopers came panting up the rocky way, and
upon reaching the position so lately occupied by the
outlaws, stood still and gazed with wonder. From

here the earth slanted down to the chasm, about twenty yards away, and towards it Stanford was rushing with incredible speed. Then, ere they had even guessed his desperate intention, they saw him bound into the air like a greyhound. The next moment he was clinging for dear life to the opposite ledge, for though he had cleared the fearful space it was yet a question whether he would be able to pull himself up over the ledge in safety. The troopers, wonderstruck, looked on with admiration. Though they had hunted him as they would a tiger, though a moment ago they would have shot him down without compunction, they could yet admire his splendid struggle for liberty.

All this time he clung to the rocks like a great lizard, and surely, surely, he was dragging himself up. Another foot and he would be able to crawl; a few yards then and the great boulders would hide him from the guns of his enemies; and all the time the troopers looked on with wonder and admiration, nor raised a gun, nor even attempted to check his progress. They might have been the spectators of some theatrical show instead of men engaged in the stern duty of life and death. But he who is heroic can appreciate heroism in others. A few minutes ago the men were literally thirsting for his blood; now they stood with wide, wondering eyes, lost in admiration of his daring.

All but one. The squatter, rifle in hand, leant

against a massive rock, not many yards from where
Devine had fallen, and watched with a cruel smile
Stanford's Herculean struggles. His white eyes
glistened. This was a triumph worth living for.
Every second of that fearful struggle was a year of
delight to him. He wished it might go on for ever, so
that he could eternally feast his eyes on such a
gratifying sight. Time after time he raised his rifle,
only to lower it again. Why should he help fate?
At any moment Stanford might fall back into the
abyss.

"By George!" growled the sergeant, "as brave a
fellow as ever lived."

By a superhuman effort Tom had drawn himself
out of danger, and the old trooper could not suppress
his admiration. Before he had time, however, to call
on Stanford to surrender, a rifle was discharged
beside him. Tom stopped, was seen to tremble, and
then clutch wildly at the rocks. For a few seconds he
maintained his position, then slipped, slipped in spite
of his desperate struggles, and the next moment fell
backwards into the abyss.

"Who fired that shot?" thundered the sergeant.

"I," cried Wingrove, with a triumphant smile.

"Then it was the work of a d——d coward!"

"Look here, Mr. Sergeant," replied the squatter, "I
would have you remember who I am; and let me tell
you, sir, that I have not been impressed with the way

in which you have carried out this business. In fact, when I return to Melbourne, I——"

These were the last words he ever spoke. In their excitement no one had paid any attention to Devine's supposed corpse. He, however, was not dead, though dying fast. The few moments of consciousness which were left him sufficed for the crowning act of this terrible drama. He, with a ghastly effort, raised himself on his elbow. He had not forgotten his promise to Tom that he would keep a shot for the squatter. Taking deliberate aim he fired, and the ball crashed through the Member's brain.

The troopers started back in amazement, then sprang forward in a body to seize the dying outlaw. With a moan the culprit sank back; the blood gushed afresh from the ragged wound in his throat; his jaw dropped. He had given up the ghost.

CHAPTER XX.

THE CURTAIN DESCENDS.

ALL that day the sick girl sat by her window in distant Koorabyn, a prey to a thousand fears. She watched the sun steal slowly round its course, saw it hang above the granite peaks of Mount Desolation, then begin to sink, sink, a world of sullen fire. By degrees the mountain assumed its dreadful demoniacal proportions—a monster from which she shrank with horror. She hid her face in her hands; she shut her eyes to hide the direful sight; but such weak subterfuges could not dispel the grim truth. There the hateful thing stood out—a sign, a hideous warning.

She called for her father. She could bear the strain no longer; neither would she be put off with further excuses. She must know how the day was going; she should die if she were kept much longer in suspense. Mr. Franklin mounted his fleetest horse and galloped off to the township. Upon his arrival there he rode direct to the police camp. The troopers had but an hour ago returned, and soon the tragic story was known. With a heavy heart he remounted and turned once more for home.

His daughter was still at the window as he rode up the well-known path. Indeed, she had not quitted that point of vantage during his entire absence; but with a passionate and despairing look had sat watching the mountain and the dusty road. As he entered the room, she saw his face was ghastly in its paleness; and when he spoke, his voice quivered painfully.

"Courage, dear," he whispered, as he took her in his arms—"courage."

"He is taken?"

"No—but——"

"He is dead?"

He pressed her to him, but spoke not. Yet there was no need for words. His silence admitted all. She looked up into his face in a dazed, half-conscious way.

"He is dead, you say—dead?"

"Yes."

All her strength seemed to forsake her. She hung limp and lifeless in his arms.

"Let me lie down," she said; "I am very tired."

For many days she hovered between life and death; then followed long weeks of convalescence; and when she was strong enough to undertake the journey, her father took her away to Melbourne.

"You shall never see Mount Desolation again," said he; and she had no wish to. Shortly after

Koorabyn was put in the market, and its new pur-
chaser little dreamt of the romantic part its late
inhabitants played in the tragedy of the Wooroota
bushrangers.

Of the doings of Stanford the history of the future
will speak in its own way; but the fact that he gave
up his all for the woman he loved, however wrong in
principle it may be, will surely soften all sympathetic
natures towards him, and may, in time, whiten his
blackest spots. In strange contrast to him stood his
friend Devine. Poor Joe was looked upon as a fiend
incarnate, and the tales the troopers told of his
savagery and daring filled many a gentle breast with
terror. Stanford was pitied, Devine execrated. The
former was the hero of countless ballads, in which his
many qualities were magnified so preposterously that
he became a sort of popular personage; the latter
was reviled as a human monster, a devil who
absolutely revelled in the sight of blood. Such is the
way of the world, and such the world's knowledge of
most things. But we who know more of him than
even the trooper who shot him down, can look on and
smile—if we feel so inclined. Earth hath no greater
love than this—that one man shall lay down his life
for another.

In the little graveyard at the foot of Mount Desolation there was placed, a twelvemonth after the

incidents herein related, a snow-white marble cross, over what had hitherto been an unnamed mound of earth. A tall slender girl, with a white sad face and great brown eyes full of unspeakable woe, had brought it with her from the capital, and having seen it placed in position, had departed as silently and sadly as she had come. The gravedigger is paid well to plant flowers round that tomb and keep the headstone in repair; and if you will advance well into the light you will read, as distinctly now as on the day when it was first erected, the legend engraven thereon.

It runs as follows :—

"T O M.

" When the Mount like a demon looms through the glare of a sullen fire,
The heart of the watcher shall weep for the loss of a soul's desire."

THE END.

PRINTED BY
CASSELL & COMPANY, LIMITED, LA BELLE SAUVAGE
LONDON, E.C.

www.ingramcontent.com/pod-product-compliance
Lightning Source LLC
Chambersburg PA
CBHW020322140726
47905CB00013B/2149

*9 7 8 3 3 3 7 3 1 5 7 6 4 *